Copyright © 2022 by Mara Webb

All rights reserved. No part of this publication may be reproduced, distributed, or transmitted in any form or by any means, including photocopying, recording, or other electronic or mechanical methods, without the prior written permission of the publisher, except in the case of brief quotations embodied in critical reviews and certain other noncommercial uses permitted by copyright law.

CHAPTER 1

I don't know if it's just me, but when I think of the words 'Magic School' a whole host of enchanting imagery comes to mind. Magnificent castles, massive stone towers, a world of wonder and majesty just waiting to be discovered.

As an adult witch I was considered a 'late-starter', so I had to play catch up at Compass Cove Community College of Magic. I'd received an acceptance letter in the mail a few weeks ago and I'd been excited ever since.

But as I parked in the small lot and got out of my van, I couldn't help but feel a little deflated as I looked upon a small one-story building with a flat roof and beige walls. "This can't be the right place…" I muttered to myself. A sign over the door said 'Aposhine Accounting', a possible sign I might be in the wrong place if I hadn't been told about it ahead of time. The sign was a deliberate fake, to 'keep the normies away'.

On my left I saw a transparent blue shape appear in my periphery and I turned to see the ghost of my Aunt Constance before she could sneak up and scare me. "Don't even try it," I warned her.

"Oh boo," she said. "I thought I'd come along and wish you good luck on your first night. Why are you standing here in the parking lot by yourself? Nervous?"

"No, I'm just wondering if I have the right place. This grim little building doesn't exactly spark one's imagination."

"Zora this is a Community College of Magic, what were you expecting? If you'd gone to magic school as a teenager, it would be slightly more exotic. There's Saint Zeboga's just thirty minutes north of here, it's a little boarding school—all the witches and wizards go."

"See? That sounds exciting! This however…" Once again, I looked at the drab concrete shack where my magic tuition would take place. "I guess I better head inside then."

Inside I found one large and mostly empty room. Two dozen seats faced a small stage, all empty except a man and woman who were talking quietly amongst themselves. As I came through the door, they both turned around to regard me.

"Are you here for the class as well?" the woman said excitedly.

"Uh…yes," I said, walking over and taking a seat behind her. I set my bag down on the chair next to me. "My name is Zora Wick."

"Jane, Jane West. Terribly excited to get started!"

"Neil Mayo, and before you ask, no, my family has nothing to do with mayonnaise."

"…Right," I said, offering him a weak smile. "Is it just the three of us then? I expected more. Where's the teacher?"

"He's already here!" a disembodied voice bellowed. A flash of white smoke erupted on stage and as it cleared away, I could see a man with his arms held out dramatically. He started coughing and fanned the smoke away. "Hello, hello! I'm Amos, Amos Aposhine! Your teacher for this term!"

Amos was a wrinkled old man with a large white beard. He wore a dark blue suit covered in white stars and moons. The twinkle in his eyes and warmth in his voice made me think of him as an eccentric grandfather character.

He looked at the seats before him and his eyes grew wide. "Wow, three of you? Big class this year. We'll have to get started right away." From his voice I detected no hint of sarcasm. "Why don't we all go around the room and introduce ourselves? I'd like you to mention how you first came upon your powers. I'll go first as example... my name is Amos, I was born in a travelling circus, and I come from a long line of magical people. My mother said I was making magic happen since I could walk, a very early starter." Amos looked at Jane and pointed at her. "You there, go!"

Jane stood up and took a few steps forward before turning around to look at me and Neil. "Hi everyone!" she said cheerily. "My name's Jane. Everyone in my family is magical, but my powers never came. Dad always said I was so special I didn't need magic like everyone else. I went to a regular mortal school and got myself a normal job—I'm a vet. Anyway, it was my 28th birthday the other day and when I went to blow out the candles on my cake, I ended up floating into the air! Mom passed out and my sisters couldn't believe it! I applied for school the next day!"

"Very good, very good!" Amos said with an enthusiastic round of applause. Neil and I joined in as well of course. "Take a seat Miss West. I've seen my fair share of late starters in here before and let me assure you there is plenty of time to catch up! Just a few years ago I had a man from an all-magical family, his powers didn't come in until he was 43! He now works for the Magic Council, just goes to show you can get places if you put the work in... you there!" Amos said, pointing at Neil. "Let's hear it!"

Neil stood up to give his introduction. "So, this magic stuff is completely new to me, everyone in my family are 'mortals', and up until a few weeks ago I thought magic was all made up. I realized something was wrong when I was driving to work one day—I'm a salesman at a tire shop—I wished the traffic would ease up and suddenly all the cars on the road slid to one side! I thought I was having a stroke..."

"What happened then?" I asked.

"Well, I arrived at work and sat down at my desk when this strange looking woman walked in wearing a bright green suit... she started lecturing me about 'Improper use of magic in public' and slapped a

$10,000 fine on my desk! I thought it was some bizarre prank until she realized I genuinely had no idea."

"Yes," Amos chipped in. "Magic Crimes Investigation are usually the first ones to pick up wizards like Neil. It's not very common that magic folk come from non-magic families, and even less common that it starts out of the blue much later in life. Once MCI realized what was going on they referred you to me Neil, and now you're here. Did you get through all the pre-term material okay?"

"I did," Neil nodded proudly. "I'm a little overwhelmed that all this crazy stuff actually exists, but I'm here, and my mind is open!"

"Brilliant," Amos said with a gentile wink. "That's all you need. Take a seat, thanks. Over to our last student. Stand up and introduce yourself!"

"Zora, Zora Wick," I said once again as I stood up. "I didn't get any pre-term materials?"

"Not to worry," Amos assured. "It's only for students that grow up without a magical family."

"But I didn't! I mean I have one now, but I only got one recently." I looked at Neil and Jane, who were staring back at me in expectation. "I uh grew up non-magical, and then I found out I have a magic family. I moved here two months ago, inherited a magical bakery, and an annoying talking cat. My dead aunt follows me around in ghost form, I've solved three murder mysteries since moving here, fought off a group of possessed merfolk, have successfully dodged a kidnap attempt from dark witches, and a werewolf and magically enhanced human have sworn their lives to protect me from danger."

A moment of silence passed over the room as the three of them stared at me. "...I don't think you need the pre-term materials," Neil said.

"Yes, it's seems you're quickly getting acquainted with our bizarre and extensive world!" Amos said emphatically. "I must admit I was excited to see your name when you applied Miss Wick, you've ended up in the paper once or twice since moving here—couldn't help but noticing."

I nodded my head. "It's been a weird few months, hopefully everything starts to quiet down a little bit now though." Though I wasn't holding my breath.

"Oh, I'm sure it will," Amos said. "Anyway, let us begin. If everyone can come and stand over here by the stage for a moment…"

After we moved Amos waved his hands and the chairs floated themselves into the corner of the room, settling in several neat stacks. Amos instructed us all to spread out and handed us each a book titled *Blundell's Bumper Book of Beginner Spells*. "Now before we begin there is one small matter of assessing what kind of witch or wizard you are and getting you a wand. Such matters are slightly outside my expertise, but luckily, I have a helper, Sabrina!"

My mouth dropped as my cousin Sabrina walked into the room. She ran a shop in town called *Wytch's Bazaar*. I knew that Sabrina was one of the only wand-makers in town, but I hadn't anticipated that I'd see her here tonight.

"Hello everyone!" she said warmly. "My name is Sabrina and I run a magic shop here in Compass Cove. I also make and sell wands. Also, I'm Zora's cousin. Hi Zora!" Sabrina waved at me, grinning like an idiot.

"You didn't tell me you were going to be here!" I said.

"Thought it'd be a nice surprise. Now, Neil, Jane, come over here and let's find you a wand and your witch type. I already sorted Zora out a few weeks ago so it shouldn't take long…"

While Sabrina dealt with Neil and Jane, Amos came over to talk to me. "Let's have a look at your wand then!" he said heartily.

When a witch or wizard wasn't using their wand, it was normal for them to store it in their 'aura' an invisible pocket of energy that surrounded your body. I placed my finger and thumb against my palm and pulled my wand out. This wasn't actually the wand Sabrina had given me when I'd gone to her shop, it was a replacement wand given to me by a Wand Insurance salesman after I'd deliberately broken my old one. It was a long story, but basically I'd done it to get a free magical top up so I could stop a mad siren queen—you know, just another regular day in Compass Cove.

"Huh…" Amos said as he took the wand and gave it a couple of swishes through the air. The replacement wand was very plain looking, a stick of bumpy white wood that looked like it had been hewn in a hurry. As Amos moved the wand a patch of multi-colored light glowed faintly under the surface.

"You can use it?!" I remarked in amazement.

"Only just about. A wand will always reveal itself to a teacher. Still, I've never seen one like this before. What are you, a divination witch?"

"Uh… Prismatic, actually," I said in a low voice. When I first moved here witch types was one of the first things I'd learned about. There were five main witch types apparently: Kitchen, Cosmic, Divination, Sea, and Green. I just happened to be a sixth type that was much rarer —A Prismatic Witch.

"Bloody hell," Amos said, his eyes growing wide as he handed the wand back. "Never had one of them before, that explains why I didn't recognize the wand! Still, that *thing* seems a little shaky to me. Did your cousin Sabrina make that?"

"No, it's a replacement, I broke my other one," I explained.

"And have you had any problems with this replacement wand?"

"No, not at all!" After a moment of reflection I added, "Wait, well…"

The truth was that there *had* been a few small hiccups with magic over the last week. I was only practicing simple magical spells at the moment, but every now and then my wand had started doing things that were completely unexpected. I had no idea what was going on, and I'd been more and more reluctant to use magic. Up until now I figured it was something to do with me, but now that I thought about it the problems had started around the same time I changed the wand.

I shared this with Amos and he nodded. "I see. Those replacements are usually cheap knock off things. I highly doubt they'd have a good replacement wand in stock for a Prismatic Witch. Very likely they bought a cheap one at the last minute when you joined their books. I'd strongly encourage you to get a real replacement quickly from Sabrina. She's a pro, she knows what she's doing."

"Finished!" Sabrina shouted from the other side of the room. Looking over I saw Neil and Jane triumphantly holding their new wands. Sabrina snapped her fingers and the stack of wand boxes behind her disappeared. "You've got yourself a divination witch Amos," she said and gestured at Jane, "And Neil here is a green witch!"

"Marvelous," Amos cheered. "We'll get started with some magic then, Neil, Jane, if you turn to page ten in your books and start reading, I'll be over in a minute. Sabrina, if we could have a word?"

Sabrina came over to Amos and me. "What's up?" she asked.

"I was just looking at Zora's replacement wand here, and it's… well, just take a look at it." Amos handed my wand to Sabrina, who hadn't studied it properly until now. After holding it for only a second she looked up at me in dismay. "Zora! You should have told me they lumped you with this! Have you been doing magic with this hunk of junk?"

"Not very well…" I admitted.

"You should have said something!"

"I didn't want to be a nuisance, and I thought maybe *I* was the one doing something wrong. It only occurred to me tonight that the wand might be at fault."

Amos looked at Sabrina. "Well, can you replace it with something more suitable?"

Sabrina scratched her head as she passed the wand back to me. "Not tonight. I only had one Prismatic wand in stock, and Zora already broke that one—with good reason of course. I can make you another, but it's not going to be easy—it's not like making a wand for regular witches… I might need some help."

"And doesn't that sound like a brilliant way to accrue some extracurricular credit?" Amos said. "Until then Sabrina, I think this current wand will do just fine. It should handle some gentle beginner magic okay, right?"

Sabrina looked unsurely at the wand. "Uh… sure," she said.

"Brilliant! Then we can begin our lessons. Thanks for all the help, Sabrina, a star as always."

After Sabrina left, we started with some basic magical exercises. The first chapter in our beginner magic books focused on conjuration and transportation. The very first task was simple—magic up a teacup and then transport it to the other side of the room using only our wands. Amos had us all take turns.

"Not bad, Jane, not bad at all. Careful as you float it across now, you don't want to—ah! Never mind, just a little lower next time. Cups tend to break when they accelerate into ceilings."

Then there was Neil, who magicked up a pint glass instead of a cup. "Never mind Neil, let's float that across instead. Excellent, excellent, now set it down gently!" With Amos' encouragement Neil *did* set his pint glass down on the floor, only for it to explode a second later out of nowhere.

"Alright Zora, now over to you. Place a cup in your mind and hold your wand steady as you say the incantation out loud!"

As I stepped up to the task, I must admit I felt overly confident. Not only had I been conjuring up things for weeks now, I'd been transporting things too. I'd even tried a little transfiguration, but that was slightly trickier.

With the image of a porcelain teacup at the front of my mind I pointed my wand at the ground and uttered the incantation. Unfortunately, the spell didn't go exactly right. A huge grey form crashed to the ground and the room shook all around me. The next thing I knew I was staring in the face of a full-sized African Rhinoceros.

For a moment I stood there frozen in fear. The most perplexing thing is that the rhino *did* have a tiny teacup balanced upside on its horn. A sharp exhale of air came from its nostrils, and it pulled its hoof across the floor.

"Uh..." I began.

"Run!" Amos shouted. "Run, run!"

I dove out of the way just as the rhino charged past me. It crashed through the exterior wall of the building and carried on into the parking lot. Amos bolted outside with his wand held high, shouting some unknown incantation at the top of his voice. *"Prohibere, Prohibere!"* he wailed.

Neil, Jane, and I got to the hole in the wall just as the rhino vanished in a cloud of magical green light. Amos, who was doubled over and out of breath, stood up and walked back over to us, wiping the back of his hand over his drenched brow.

"Perhaps you get that wand sorted out sooner than later?" Amos rasped.

"Sorry," I mumbled. "That's never happened before."

"Quite alright, quite alright," he said, his eyes warily regarding the wand. "I think we'll leave it there for tonight." Neil raised his hand gingerly. "Yes, Neil?"

"In all fairness sir it *did* have a teacup on its horn."

Amos blinked as he considered the point. "Yes, Neil, I suppose it did. Uh, good job, Zora."

I looked at the bits of wall scattered across the parking lot and wished the earth would swallow me whole. "I think we have different definitions of a good job."

CHAPTER 2

*D*aphne and Zelda were doubled over in fits of laughter as I shared my wand malfunction. Zelda had a day off from the café, but she'd decided to come over and help out with the morning set up.

"I'm sorry Zora, I know I shouldn't laugh, but how do you keep landing yourself in these situations?"

"I have a theory that I'm cursed by a gypsy... is that a thing?" I posited. "Sabrina said it's not going to be easy sorting out a new wand too. I'll have to swing around at some point and see what has to be done."

"Wand malfunctions happen to everyone at some point," Daphne said in an effort to make me feel better. "Once in school I accidentally blasted all the windows out of the greenhouse during a herbology class. I was 'glass girl' for the rest of school!"

"Wait, that was you?" Zelda said, straightening up a little. "There was a 'glass girl' a few years below me."

Daphne held her hand up, admitting to the title. "That's me, the one and only. I have some signed t-shirts in the trunk of my car if you're interested, photos are $20," she joked.

"Speaking of signed t-shirts..." Zelda began. "Actually, I can't make that segue at all. Zora, you had a date the other night and you've been expertly avoiding all questions about it."

"Yes, there's a reason for that," I said as I rolled out some dough. "I don't want to talk about it." Daphne sniggered at my bluntness.

"Oh, come on! Blake actually took you out for a real-life date to an ice rink! That's *so* romantic. What happened, give us the details, I'm dying!" Zelda threw her hands up in the air dramatically.

"We had a lot of fun, I nearly rolled my ankle, then I went home. That's about the long and short of it."

"Do you like him?" Daphne asked. She wasn't as annoying or persistent as Zelda, so I didn't feel as reluctant to answer her questions.

"I... don't know."

Truthfully, I was actually starting to like both Blake *and* Hudson, the two men that had deemed themselves as my magical protectors. They were both unapologetic alpha males, and they both hated each other too. I'd been avoiding talking about both of them, and it was partly because I was worried sick about Hudson—who had been missing for two weeks now.

When I last saw him, it was a surprise visit. He worked for a secret magical organization, and he came to tell me was going on a dangerous mission, one with low odds of survival. Right before he left, he kissed me, an action that had left me feeling dizzy and euphoric.

I didn't know when he was meant to be back, and part of me thought he'd come back no problem, but with each passing day I felt myself worrying more.

During his absence Blake took me out ice skating, it wasn't officially a 'date' or anything, just two friends doing something fun together. At the end of the not-date he'd surprised me by kissing me too.

I wasn't exactly tied to either of the men, but with my heart spinning in all directions, I had no idea what I was meant to do. I hadn't told anyone about the kisses because everyone in my life was an absolute gossip, and I knew that if Blake or Hudson found out the other one had made a move, they'd have some big blow up about it.

"She's hiding something." Zelda looked at me shrewdly while scooping frosting into a piping bag. "I can feel it!"

"I'm not hiding anything; now can we hurry and get this morning prep finished? We open in five minutes!"

"What's Zora hiding now?" my familiar Hermes asked as he walked into the kitchen. The little black cat hopped onto his designated stool, sat down and licked the back of his paw.

"Blake and Hudson," Zelda said. "What's going on with them?"

"Blake took her ice-skating; Hudson is possibly dead?" Hermes said.

"Yes, we already know all that." Daphne sliced a tray bake into neat little squares. "You're not telling us anything new."

"What, like the fact that she kissed them both?" Hermes purred casually.

"Hermes!" I gasped.

Both Zelda and Daphne had stopped what they were doing, massive smiles plastered across their faces. "I knew it!" Zelda roared.

"Zora and Blake and Hudson, sitting in a tree..." Daphne sang, woefully out of time.

"I did *not* do that," I said to Daphne and Zelda.

"Your reaction tells me otherwise," Zelda cackled.

I turned at Hermes and shot daggers at him. "How did you even know?"

"You talk in your sleep," Hermes said. "And I *listen*." He added that last part with a wink.

"Creepy," Zelda muttered. Just a little bit.

"For the record *they* both kissed me, and I'm keeping it secret because if either of one of them finds out they'll start another punch up with each other."

"Why can't I be trapped in some steamy love triangle?" Daphne said wistfully. "Life's not fair."

"Uh at least you had a date recently," Zelda offered. "The last time a guy stared into my eyes I was having them tested. He is a bit old, and I think he was just doing his job, but..."

"Bad Zelda, stop it," I said, flicking her ears. "There are plenty of nice men out there for both of you. Things aren't so desperate that you have to entertain the idea of lusting after your geriatric optician. We *will* find someone for both of you."

"That's if Zora doesn't snap them all up first," Hermes cracked. He jumped off the stool and ran out of the kitchen as I jumped over to swipe at him playfully. "Too slow, too slow!" he guffawed.

After the morning baking—and gossip—were all out of the way we opened up the shop and served our steadily growing stream of regulars. The first couple of hours passed by rather quickly because things were so busy. Zelda went home at lunch to leave Daphne and us to it. Thankfully the majority of our customers were pleasant to deal with and I really loved interacting with them in the mornings. There were usually one or two odd characters, but as a whole my mood was bright—even if my deadly secrets had slipped out thanks to Hermes.

Midway through the afternoon however my mood took a turn as an unexpected customer came into the shop. We were having a quiet moment when three large bodyguards came in, followed by a man in leathers and sunshades. He had the intolerable swagger of a man that thought himself to be very important. As he surveyed the shop he walked up to the counter and stopped in front of Daphne.

"Do you know who I am?" he said, tipping his shades down slightly so he could look over them. I was in the back at first so I only heard his voice, but as I came into the shop I saw him and recognized him at once.

"Yes!" squeaked Daphne. "You're Patrick Black!"

I had to admit I wasn't really 'down' with celebrity culture, and if a famous person walked into my shop, I wouldn't know them nine times out of ten. Patrick Black, however, was another matter altogether. Not only was he one of the most famous rock stars on the planet, but I actually dug his music too.

"You're god damn right, so let's get a few things clear. No one knows I was in here, *period*. Is that clear?" As I looked past Patrick

Black, I realized his three bodyguards had blocked the entrance to the shop. No one else was trying to get in at the moment, but if they wanted to, they wouldn't be able. "Who's in charge?"

"That would be me, Zora Wick," I said firmly. "How may I help you?"

Black looked over at me and considered me for a moment. "Well Miss Wick, I'm happy to reveal that you've been chosen for an exciting business venture. I'm hosting a party at my new mansion in the hills this week, and I require the services of your bakery."

"We can cater," I said, "but an event at the last moment will have to be charged at a premium—"

Patrick Black pulled out a roll of banknotes and slapped them down onto the counter. "There's $10,000. I trust that's enough to hear no more objections?"

My mouth opened and closed momentarily as I considered my response. I didn't exactly like the attitude he was giving, but that amount of money would be very good for the bakery. "So, what do you need?" I asked.

Black smiled upon getting his way. He pulled out his phone and, on the screen, there was a picture of a pretty Japanese girl. "Who is this?" he asked.

"Uh…" I had no idea.

"Ana Akoto!" Daphne swooned. "She's only like the biggest pop star at the moment!"

"Try the biggest pop star of *all time*," Patrick Black corrected. "She's going to be at my party, flying all the way from japan—and I want to make her mine. Here's the thing, she's very into this cute little bakery thing." Black waved his hand over the counters. "I had my assistant do some research and apparently this place is the best in town."

"We uh… we strive to serve perfection every time," I said. I was mostly caught off-guard at having earned that apparent reputation.

"It's very important that I impress her. Everything needs to be perfect. I want her to come into my room and find those little cake stands with an offering of every item you make. Can you do that?"

"Like a tea party?" I asked. "We can do that, but it normally only costs $200." I looked at the fat roll of notes on the counter. "For that amount of money, I expected you might want more."

Black took his shades off fully now and looked at me. "Would you rather have a table full of subpar products, or a small selection of the very best?"

"Well, I'm a glutton, so—" I began to joke but Black interrupted me.

"My terms are clear. Deliver the goods tomorrow night and you've earned the money in my eyes." Black put his shades back on and then looked at Daphne. He glanced back at his bodyguard. "Mike, get Francesca in here."

The bodyguard went outside and came back with a gangly brunette woman wearing a fancy business dress. "Patrick?" she asked.

"This one?" he hazarded, pointing at Daphne. 'Francesca' also looked at Daphne and nodded.

"Good cheekbones, yes," she agreed. Francesca stepped forward to Daphne. "Do you want a picture with Patrick Black? We can send you an autographed copy."

"Yes!" Daphne blurted. 'Francesca' also looked at me.

"You're not bad either. Would you like one too?"

"Not bad?" I asked.

"She means pretty," Patrick said bluntly. "I don't take photographs with ugly chicks."

"Oh..." I said with abhorrent realization. "I'm actually camera shy, so no thanks," I lied.

"Suit yourself. Let's get the picture then."

Daphne came around the front of the counter and posed next to Patrick while Francesca got a camera ready.

"You may hold his arm," Francesca directed. "Look like you're madly in love with him. That's right. Perfect."

I couldn't help noticing that during the pose Patrick Black put on a very deliberate expression, he looked away from Daphne, almost as if he was disgusted to stand next to her... even though the photo op was his idea.

'What are they up to?' I thought to myself.

"Brilliant! We'll send a copy in the post," Francesca announced. "Patrick we have to get going, you have rehearsals at three."

Francesca gave me the details of the party, the entourage left the shop, and a very giddy Daphne skipped back around the counter, thoroughly delighted about her celebrity encounter. "He was amazing!" she praised.

"He was something alright..." I muttered to myself. I took the fat stack of notes and put it in the safe. "Still, that money is going to come in mighty helpful. We'll probably have to start a little earlier on the day that we have extra to do. Do you want to take the rest of the afternoon off? It's looking a little quiet now anyway."

"Ooh, could I? I might go and get my hair done ahead of this job. We're going to Patrick Black's mansion! Patrick Black has a mansion in town!" Daphne was bouncing up and down with excitement.

"Yeah... listen, Zelda and the girls are coming around tonight for Chinese food and a movie, or something. You want to come too?"

"Sure, see you later!" Daphne said as she grabbed her jacket. "Patrick Black, Zora. Patrick Black! Can you believe it?!"

After Daphne left, I tidied up most of the kitchen while serving the trickle of customers before I closed up for the day. Upstairs in my apartment I told Hermes about the star encounter, and he didn't seem too bothered.

"Never heard of him. What does he sing?"

"He's in a band, *Midnight Crow Explosion*. They're like super big, and they have so many good songs."

"Well how come you're so calm then? If this guy is so famous."

"I admit I was fangirling a little bit when he first came in, but he was kind of rude, so that tarnished my opinion of him a little."

"You know back in my day I was pretty famous too. They called me the 'Unmatchable Hermes!'. People came from far and wide to watch me—"

"Every time you tell this story it's a different adjective. First it was the 'Great Hermes!' then it was the 'Amazing Hermes!', so which one is it?"

Hermes looked at me like I'd just slapped him in the face. "They called me lots of different things. Do you want to hear the story or not?"

"Yes, please, go on," I said sarcastically.

"No, you know what, I don't want to tell it now. You can sit in silence!" Hermes jumped down from the table and strutted off towards the bedroom. The doorbell rang as he left the room.

"That'll be the girls here to disrupt my silence," I said loudly, making sure Hermes would hear. It always amused me when he got into his little moods. As I opened the door Zelda, Celeste and Sabrina all rushed in, boxes of Chinese food in their arms.

"Settle an argument, Zora!" Zelda said as she dumped the boxes of Chinese food onto the table. "How many smurfs could fit inside a suitcase?"

"This is seriously what you guys have been arguing about on the way over here?" I groaned while shutting the door.

"Just say more than a hundred and we can drop it!" Zelda swished her fringe out of her face.

"She's not going to say that, because it's *insane*," Sabrina countered. "No way you could fit more than a hundred in."

"You're staying strangely quiet," I said to Celeste.

"Because they're both wrong, the question is pointless. Smurfs aren't stupid, they wouldn't hop into a suitcase like that."

"And here I thought you were about to say something normal," I said.

"It's theoretical, Celeste!" Sabrina wailed. "What's so hard to understand?! Zora, what do you think?"

"I'm thinking I should have had a quiet night to myself. Is it too late to kick you guys out?"

"If we go, the food goes too," Zelda said, shoving a spring roll into her mouth.

"...I guess you can stay then! Now, what kind of suitcase are we talking about?"

CHAPTER 3

The next day I took a morning off from the bakery to take care of some chores. I did help Daphne get everything set up for the morning, but when the sign flipped to open, I went out to take care of business. At about lunchtime I had caught up with everything I wanted to sort out, so I decided to pay Zelda and Celeste a visit and see how things were going in their café.

I was just about to walk inside when Zelda came out, she was wearing a small backpack.

"Hey, I just came to—"

"Got to run to the bank, come with me!" Zelda said, pulling my hand as she set off down the sidewalk.

"I was hoping to sit down and have a drink actually…"

"Eh you'll survive, so how has your morning been?" she asked.

"Oh, you know, full of chores. How's the café?"

"Super busy. Celeste and I have been staring through the windows all morning, hoping we might catch sight of this rock star friend of yours."

Our little celebrity encounter had inevitably come up last night, and so had the gossip about Blake and Hudson. The girls had a whale of a time making fun of me for that one. Why I still invited them around regularly I'll never know.

"I don't think he's going to be walking down the street in broad daylight—he'd get mobbed within an inch of his life!"

"Especially now that he's single," Zelda said with shock as her eyes fell upon a newspaper stand in front of us. I hadn't yet seen today's newspaper, but as I read the headline my mouth fell open.

"That slimy, sniveling, screwball!" I gasped. Running over to the newspaper I picked it up, my hands shaking as I read the article. In giant words above the photograph taken yesterday of Patrick Black and Daphne, the headline read: BLACK BREAKS UP WITH DESPERATE PSYCHO-EX.

'In the early hours of this morning the Compass Cove Bugle learned that Patrick Black has called things off with his most recent girlfriend, pictured above. The breakup was prompted after Black's ex reportedly assaulted him after demanding a baby from Black. We have it on good authority that Black's ex has now been taken into custody and is awaiting sentencing...'

"Unbelievable!" I roared.

"Who are you calling?" Zelda asked as I pulled my phone out of my pocket.

"I'm calling the paper! How dare they print this! Not a word of it is true!" I dialed the number for the paper and scanned the article to see who had authored this steaming pile of trash. My eyes settled on the name *Carla King,* and I wasn't surprised. I'd already had a run in with Carla after she'd printed a false story about me, alluding that I was a murderer.

"Compass Cove Bugle," Carla answered after one ring.

"How very dare you run that tripe in the paper! It's not true!"

"Which story are you referring to?"

"The frontpage story! About Black and his girlfriend!"

"Oh," Carla chuckled. "Yes, that's a publicity piece. Black's agent himself gave it to us. They pay us to put those stories in the paper. Say, do I know your voice from somewhere?"

"Wick! Zora Wick! You ran another lie several weeks ago claiming I was a murderer!"

"Zora!" Carla said with an air of amiable familiarity. "How have you been? We should get a coffee some time. I could run a small story about your booming café!"

"I'd rather stick my head in a bucket of fleas!"

I hung up the phone and tried to steady my breathing. I was so angry that Black and his agent would do something like this to Daphne.

"Come on," Zelda said. "Let me sort out this bank thing and we'll get a drink. Celeste said I can take the rest of the afternoon off!"

While Zelda went into the bank, I took out my phone again and called Blake at the police station. "Zora!" he said. "I was just thinking about you."

"Someone has to do something about the Compass Cove Bugle. They're printing lies again!"

Blake chuckled. "From what I've heard that's pretty much all the print. What are they saying about you now?"

"Not me, it's about my friend." I brought Blake up to speed and he listened intently.

"Ah, I see. Famous guys like that will do anything to keep their names in the paper, even if it means dashing the reputations of others. Listen I've been meaning to talk to you actually, I feel like things have been distant between us ever since the date, and I just wanted to make sure I didn't overstep my mark, I mean—"

"Things are fine, Blake, really. I'm just trying to process everything. Why don't you come on over and we can talk about it? I'm not sure where my head is at the moment."

"Uh oh, that doesn't sound good," he remarked.

"It's not like that. It's just… there's something I need to tell you." It was kind of eating me alive that I was caught between Blake and Hudson, and I didn't want to keep secrets any longer. To make matters worse every time I thought about Hudson, I felt more worried, and I had no way of contacting him.

Or did I?

"Oh, okay? Well, I'll come around later. Bye then."

Zelda came back out of the bank just as I ended the call. "All done! Want to get a drink?"

"Sure, but let's make it to go. I need to find out if Hudson is okay, and I think I might have a way of finding out. We should probably go and give Daphne a heads up on this story first though."

We walked back to the bakery and gave Daphne the grim news. She was a little shocked by it, but to my surprise she took it quite well too. "You know it might not be that bad? If anything, it gives me a little street cred."

"You're not ticked off about this?" I asked her in surprise. "I was furious!"

Daphne shrugged. "I mean I'm pretty annoyed, but I try not to care too much about what other people are saying about me. I mean hello, glass girl here, I had to grow a pretty thick skin after years of taunting!"

"You're a bigger person than I am. I'm all for throwing this jerk's money back in his face and cancelling the job, just give me the word."

Daphne batted her hand dismissively. "Nope, don't be ridiculous. I'm not bothered about the story at all. Just wait until I tell my sister, she'll find it hilarious!"

Feeling relieved that Daphne was okay, Zelda and I took the van and drove out east, heading in the direction of the old burned-out arcade. From the outside it looked like a long-abandoned wreck, but I knew it was one of Hudson's secret hideouts. We'd been here recently after he helped us with a merfolk problem.

"Wow, McNally's!" Zelda said fondly as I parked the van in the empty lot. "I've not been in here since I was a kid. Why would Hudson be here?"

"Hudson has a secret base here; you've been twice in the last month. He blanks our minds after we leave because of 'MAGE protocol'—it doesn't work on me for some reason."

"...Oh," Zelda said after a moment of reflection. "I don't remember coming here."

"You wouldn't!" I sighed. "Just follow me."

We both climbed out of the van and walked across the lot to the abandoned arcade. I didn't really have a way of getting inside, but if my suspicions were correct, I wouldn't need to. As I came up the door, I tried it and sure enough it was locked. I looked around quickly and then pulled out my wand.

"Uh... if this is a secret magic facility then should we be really breaking in here?" Zelda asked.

"Relax, we're not actually going to break in. Hudson said this place is protected by all sorts of alarms and magic. I'm planning on getting caught."

Zelda stared at me. "Cool... so you have lost your mind then, righto."

I pointed my wand at the locked door and decided to try a simple unlock charm I'd learned this week. *"Aperta!"* I said firmly. My wand glowed bright with light and started shaking. The door didn't unlock, but a long trail of bright pink sludge oozed out the end of my wand.

"Gross!" Zelda stepped back. "What is that?!"

"That looks like a highly defective wand if you ask me," someone behind us said. Zelda and I both turned with a start and saw a woman wearing a bright green dress suit. A portal was glowing in the air behind her. "Mind telling me what you're doing here?"

"My name is Zora Wick, I'm looking for Hudson."

"I know who you are," the woman said with a shrewd smile. "I assigned Hudson to look after you."

"Who are you?" I asked.

"...You can call me Monty," she said after a long pause. 'Monty' looked at my sister. "And this is Zelda Wick, your associate in mischief."

Zelda cleared her throat and laughed nervously. "In my defense she doesn't share these hare-brained schemes with me ahead of time."

"Look, I just want to know if Hudson is okay," I said to the mysterious woman. "The last time I saw him he said he might not come back. Do you know anything?"

Monty stared at me for a long hard moment before her expression eased. "He came back, three days ago. He was... in a very bad state. Fortunately, our facilities are second to none, and he's well on the road to recovery. I expect he will be discharged later today. I'll let him know you were looking for him once he's good to go."

"Let me see him now," I said. "I want to see him."

Monty shook her head. "I'm afraid that's not possible and given that you seem strangely immune to our mind-blanking technology, it would be a far greater risk letting you inside the HQ again. Now if you were interested in signing up as an agent…"

"I've already got enough on my plate. I'm not interested."

"Then I guess this conversation ends here. Hudson is alive and well. I'll pass the message on. And Zora? Don't try to break into one of our facilities again—the next meeting won't be so cordial."

"And this one was so rosy," I said.

Monty looked at Zelda. "What's that in front of your face?"

"Hm?" Zelda said, trying to find whatever Monty was referring to. The green-suited woman snapped her fingers in front of Zelda's eyes and a shower of blue sparks filled the air—it was the mind blanking spell again.

"Until next time, Zora Wick," Monty said. She walked back through the portal, and it closed. Once she was gone Zelda broke out of her temporary magical stupor.

"McNally's!" Zelda said fondly. "I've not been in here since I was a kid."

"For the love of…" I sighed to myself. "Come on, let's get out of here."

* * *

That evening Zelda and I were playing a boardgame in my apartment when there was a knock at the door. I got up and checked the buzzer to find that it was Blake.

"I'll uh… go and do something in another room," Zelda said, making herself scarce. I buzzed Blake in and he came into the kitchen, looking a little at odds with himself.

"Hey," he said. I don't think I'd ever seen him look this nervous before. "How was your day?"

"It was a normal level of whacky, which is rare these days. How about you?"

"Pretty tame. Had to arrest some drunk guy for streaking on the tube, but apart from that things were pretty normal."

I laughed and couldn't help noticing the awkward tension between us. "Uh, do you want to sit down? We can talk at the table if you like."

"Sure, that'd be great."

We both took a seat at the table. "Oh! Do you want a drink?"

"No, I'm good thanks. I'll probably head home after this; I'm feeling pretty beat. So listen, when I kissed you that was—"

"Stop," I said. "There's something I need to tell you first, something that I've been keeping from you."

A concerned expression came over Blake's face. "Oh? Okay then. Go ahead."

"Before we went on our date I bumped into—"

"Hudson," my owl Phoebe announced from her cage.

"Yeah, thanks, Phoebe, I'll tell the story myself though, yeah?"

"No, Hudson. He's at the door."

Sure enough the door buzzed, signaling that Hudson was indeed here. *Oh crap.*

I saw Blake bristle. "Hudson? He's back? You didn't tell me he was coming here. You set this up?"

"No, I didn't know he was coming. I haven't seen him since he left. Sit down and let me get the door, it's probably better to do it this way." Yeah, there would probably be no downside in telling both Hudson and Blake that I've kissed both of them and kept it secret. I headed to the door, making a mental image of the apartment for the redecoration after the inevitable brawl.

I opened the door and saw Hudson standing there, the same as the day he left. He looked a little cut up and bruised, but he was he here. He was alive. I threw my arms around him and felt this weight disappear off my shoulders. "You're alive!" I breathed.

"I'm alive," he winced. "Not completely recovered yet, but… mission accomplished. Monty told me you were looking for me. Figured I'd come and say hi." As I pulled away Hudson saw Blake sitting at the dining room table. His jaw tensed and I felt his posture stiffen. "What's he doing here?"

"So there's something I need to tell you both, and I guess this accidental reunion is as good as place as any. Come in and sit down, and no fighting—both of you."

Hudson came in and we all sat down at the table. You could cut the tension in the air with a knife.

"What the hell happened to you?" Blake remarked, seeing Hudson in his beat-up state.

"Occupational hazard. I'll be fine by tomorrow," Hudson said tersely. Blake just shook his head in response.

"Okay, let's get it out of the way then," I said. "And if either of you throws a punch in here, we are *done*. I don't want to see either of you ever again."

"Not quite the warm welcome back I was expecting," Hudson said with a genial smile.

"There's no easy way to say it, so let's just get it out in the open: you've both kissed me."

Instantly they both stood up, pushing their chairs back sharply.

"What?" Hudson said, his eyes fixed on Blake.

"What?" Blake growled back.

I dropped my head into my hand and sighed. "Sit down, both of you, I told you I don't want any punches throwing in here—"

"Best take it outside then," Blake said.

"For once we agree on something," Hudson replied.

Before anything else could happen, the door buzzed again. I looked over at Phoebe to see who it was. She stared vacantly into the distance for a second and shook her head. "I can't see, they're blocking me! It's for Zelda though... well, *both* of you actually."

"Zelda!" I called. "Someone's at the door for you!"

Zelda came sprinting out of the spare bedroom and stopped upon seeing Blake and Hudson seconds away from killing one another. Her eyes went wide. "Oh no... you told them, didn't you?"

"Just get the door, I'll sort this out."

Zelda went over to get the door but it burst open on its own as she was halfway there. A stout old woman in an old paisley dress and combat boots stepped inside the apartment and looked around with a cantankerous scowl. One eye was behind a black pirate patch, and on her back there was a rifle nearly as big as she was.

I knew this woman only in passing as Zelda's grandmother on her father's side. Nana Bucktooth, a hillbilly bandit boss with a reputation that was almost as big as her gun. Even Blake and Hudson put aside their drama to regard the woman and her dramatic entrance.

"Maw Maw!" Zelda gasped. "What are you doing here?! The treaty!"

"To hell with the treaty!" she said in her southern drawl and spat on the floor. *Nice.* "I told you I want your help! One week I said! And it's been three weeks since I last saw you!"

"Well, I've been busy—"

Nana Bucktooth repeated the words in a childish voice. "Well, I've been busy, blah blah! I don't give a hoot! You've been gone too long girl, and your family needs you now! Now stand there a minute and be quiet!"

The old woman marched into the apartment and stopped in front of the table. She took one look at Blake and Hudson and scowled. "What's going on here? Lover's tiff?"

"That's not quite—" Blake began—mistakenly so.

"Boy did I say you could speak? I don't care what you and your boyfriend are arguing about!" Nana Bucktooth snapped.

"We're not boy—" Hudson started.

"You deaf too?!" the old woman fired at Hudson. I'm not here to speak to you. It's her!"

Nana Bucktooth jabbed a finger in my direction. The little old woman had a strange and terrifying way of commanding a room. All eyes were on her, and I felt compelled to listen. "M-Me?" I stammered.

"Yeah, you! Cartwheeling all over town, causing all sorts of trouble. You and Zelda owe me, and I'm calling in the favor now."

"Since when did I owe you a favor?" I asked.

"Since you moved to this town," Nana Bucktooth said bluntly. "This lake and all the towns around it are mine, you understand?

Nothing here would be here, if it weren't for me! Your family—" Again she spat on the floor, "Owe me their lives as well, so I figure asking one little measly favor of you is actually a pretty fair bargain."

"Okay, let's hear it then. What is it you need help with?"

"Moon Juice," she said, as though that said everything I needed to know.

"Moon Juice?" I asked.

"Yup, Moon Juice. Someone's been stealing it, and I want you and Zelly over there to figure out who the culprit is."

I let out a long and drawn-out sound as I tried to navigate this conversation. "Uh… you mean like moon shine?"

Nana Bucktooth stared at me like I'd just dipped my finger in her tea. "Are you slow girl? You don't know what Moon Juice is?"

"She's still new Maw," Zelda said from across the room in my defense. "I ain't told her about the family business." One small hilarious thing about Zelda is that her country bumpkin accent slipped out whenever her family from Wildwood was around—tonight was no exception.

Nana Bucktooth looked from Zelda to me. "Moon Juice, you idiot, it's a very common ingredient for cauldron mixing. The Brewer family is the inventors and only living manufacturers! Problem is someone is stealing from me, and I need you to find out who—Moon Juice is very dangerous in the wrong hands."

"Why do you think *we* can figure this out?"

"You don't think I haven't seen you in the paper? Poking your nose in everyone's business? You'll figure it out, and if you don't—then that'll be your problem too!"

This woman, jeez.

"Listen, it's very nice to meet you properly and all, but I'm a little busy with something else here, so if you could just—"

"These love birds?!" Nana Bucktooth said, turning her attention back on Hudson and Blake. "What's the problem? Let me guess? He's not giving you enough attention? He doesn't listen enough? I ain't got a problem with homosexuals, but the drama you—"

"I think you're getting the wrong end of the stick," Hudson interrupted. "This is between us and Zora."

A light of recognition came on in the old woman's eye. "Ah... I get it now. Playing them off each other, eh Wick?" She threw her head back and cackled. "I used to do the same thing when I was young. Well... you know what they say? Absence makes the heart grow stronger. I always thought that was a load of codswallop though. I've got a fix for this... easy enough."

Without warning the old woman produced a battered looking wand, pointed it at Blake and Hudson and roared an incantation.

"Simul uten!"

A blast of air swept through the room and Nana Bucktooth disappeared her wand. With no apparent change having come over anyone we all looked around in confusion.

"Uh, what was that?" Blake asked.

"Joining curse. You're both stuck together now until I break it. You can't get further than ten feet from the other. Ha!" Again, the old woman threw her head back and cackled.

Blake and Hudson both looked horrified, and Hudson stepped back to test the theory. Sure enough he crashed against some invisible barrier and could move no further.

"No!" he shouted.

"No, no!" Blake shouted as well. "Undo it! I can't be trapped with this idiot!"

"I have a job to do!" Hudson said. "I can't be tethered to this moron!"

"You know I think a little forced proximity is the best thing here. Give you both a chance to work out your differences, what do you think?"

I looked at the mad old witch. "With all due respect ma'am, I really don't think this is going to end well."

"Oh?" she said, her brows raising on her creased forehead. "Well then let's make a deal. You help me out with my problem, and I remove the joining curse on your boyfriends here. If you ask me, it's a good way to work out their differences, but on the other hand they might just kill each other, so what do I know?"

Nana Bucktooth started back in the direction of the door, satisfied with the chaos she had wrought upon the world. Zelda said nothing but watched in silence as the old woman walked past her.

"I expect to see you in the next few days. I wouldn't want to come all the way over here again and visit—who knows what I might do next time."

"We'll come and see you in Wildwood," I said. "Another visit won't be necessary."

A toothy grin spread over the old woman's face. "Brilliant. Be seeing you Zora. Be seeing you Zelly."

"Bye Maw Maw," Zelda grumbled as Nana Bucktooth left the apartment.

"Well…" I said in the resulting silence. "She was interesting."

"Break this curse now," Blake said to me. "I can't be stuck near him."

"No one but Maw Maw can break it," Zelda said. "She's… kind of a pro when it comes to curses."

"You heard Zelda," I said, feeling slightly amused by Blake and Hudson's mutual plight. "I guess you're going to have to put aside your differences and learn to get on. Or kill each other… whichever happens first."

The two men stared fire at one another. "I'm not a betting man, but I know what I'd put my money on," Hudson said firmly.

I stared at the front door, which Nana Bucktooth had left wide open after kicking it in. I had to give it to the old woman… she knew how to make an entrance.

CHAPTER 4

I'd just taken the first sip of my morning tea when my phone started buzzing on the kitchen table. Groggily I picked it up and answered.

"M'hello?" I mumbled.

"You better be up and ready to go," Patrick Black snapped down the line. "My party is in ten hours' time, and I want those stupid little pastries waiting and ready in my room."

"You know you've got some nerve speaking to me like that after what you did to my friend? How dare you drag her name through the papers like that. All for a made-up story?" I was awake now, that was for sure.

"That's the one thing you normies will never understand. That stupid article gave me five percent bump in album sales for this dreary little town. Everyone will forget about it in a week, your friend will be fine. You obviously don't have a problem with it, you're still willing to do the job."

"Actually, I was going to give the money back and throw you out, but Daphne was pretty insistent we carried on. She's a better person than I am."

"Yawn," Patrick Black said down the phone. "I'm sorry, does it sound like I care? I want you up and baking now, if those things aren't ready for tonight there will be trouble. Everything has to be perfect for Ana Akoto."

"Don't worry, everything will be perfect for your girlfriend, though you're going to need more than pastries to win her over with your personality."

Black laughed down the phone. "I'll give it to you, not a lot of people have the balls to speak to me like that. Now are you baking the stupid cakes or not?"

"If I bake them now it'll all look like crap by the time the party rolls around. I've got them scheduled for later, don't worry, you'll have your just desserts." *Heh.*

"One more thing, if you ever talk to me like—"

"Oops!" I said as I hung up my phone and turned it off. Hermes, who was hoovering up a bowl of cat food as fast as he could, looked up at me and licked his lips.

"That guy is an impressive level of douchebag."

"Yeah, it would be funny if it wasn't happening to me. Where were you last night, anyway? You missed a whole lot of drama. Nana Bucktooth showed up, and she stuck Blake and Hudson with a joining curse."

Hermes looked pained to miss it. "Ah! You're kidding. I love that crazy old broad, she's freaking insane! Did you help Blake and Hudson out with the curse?"

"What can I do?" I asked.

"You're a Prismatic Witch, your powers would cancel out hers easily."

"It's quite possible, but I don't know the first thing about curses, and... watch this." I pulled my wand out and pointed it at a blank spot on the kitchen floor. "How about we magic up a small glass of milk?"

I pointed my wand at the floor and a violent charge swept through its bumpy wooden body. The next thing a huge hole the size of a dinner plate appeared in the floor. I stood up and looked through it, able to see clearly into the bakery kitchen below.

Hermes came over to inspect the hole too. "Wow, yeah, it's definitely time to sort that out. You could kill someone with that thing. I knew this guy once in the middle ages, great wizard called Joe—he was a wheat farmer. Joe had a great talent, but he was using this old hand-me-down wand and that thing had been fixed more than an Irish horserace!"

"Easy now," I said. "My dad was Irish. What happened to your friend?"

"Joe was out in the field one day when his plough broke. He pulled out his wand to fix it and—*poof!*—he disappeared."

"Where did he go to?"

"Get this, we didn't see him for two years, then one day he strolls back into the village. He was missing one foot, two hands, and his nose."

"Jumping jack rabbits... what happened to him?"

"The wand only went and transported him to the top of Mount Everest. Joe nearly died making his way back home. Lost the hands, foot, and nose to frost bite. We didn't have planes or cars in those days see, so he had to walk back—which took longer on account of him having only one foot."

I stared at my wand which I had placed on the kitchen table. Pink slime was oozing from the tip once more, and it felt like static energy was building up around the wand. "Yeah... I might get this sorted today. I'll give Sabrina a call."

On my way over to the flamingo phone it started ringing. "It's Sabrina," Phoebe the owl yawned from her cage.

"Ah, just the person!" I said as I picked up the phone. "I was just going to call you."

"Fancy that. I'm calling about sorting out your wand. What did *you* want to talk about?"

"Great minds think alike evidently. My current wand is a few spells away from blowing me to high heaven. How do we sort out a new one?"

"Meet me at my shop in fifteen minutes and put your hiking boots on. We're going to Fog Death Forest," Sabrina said.

"Excuse me? Did you just say Fog Death Forest? Why on earth do you think I'd feel compelled to go to a place named that?!"

"You want a new wand, don't you?"

"Well yeah," I said as I twisted the phone cord around my finger. "I thought we'd be going to witch IKEA or something though."

Sabrina just laughed. "Afraid not cuz. Maybe bring Hermes too, because this place can be pretty dangerous."

"Really? Fog Death forest can be pretty dangerous?" I said sarcastically. "I'd read such glowing reviews online."

"Don't worry, we'll have backup. Celeste and Zelda are coming too."

Sabrina had rallied all the troops evidently. Just what exactly were we walking into here?

* * *

When I arrived at Sabrina's shop Celeste and Zelda were already there. "Who's watching the café?" I asked them as I walked in.

"Roman," they both said at the same time. I had to pause upon hearing the name.

"I'm sorry, who?"

"Roman," Celeste said plainly. "He's my other employee, he covers the 3rd shift."

"How have I never met this guy?"

Celeste shrugged. "I don't know, you spend an awful lot of time galivanting around town getting into trouble." Sabrina and Zelda laughed.

"She's got a point," Zelda said.

"Spend a day in my shoes, it's not like I want to get into all this nonsense." I looked over at Sabrina. "So why are we going to 'Fog Death forest?'"

"Get in the car, I'll explain on the way. Did you bring Hermes?"

I opened my bag, in which Hermes was currently sleeping peacefully. "He's here and raring to go."

Sabrina locked up her shop and we all climbed into the bakery van. I drove while Sabrina and Celeste took the passenger seats. Zelda sat in the back with Hermes. "You want to take the road heading west out of town, I'll direct you once you're on the highway."

I took the road going out of town and a few minutes later the interstate was under our wheels. "It is safe leaving Compass Cove like this? We've still got the whole dark witch issue going on."

"We're voluntarily going into Fog Death Forest," Sabrina said. "Dark witches are the least of our problems right now."

"This place really *is* dangerous then?"

"It's a magical forest, there are magical boundaries set up all around it to stop humans from accidentally setting foot inside. There are a lot of strange things inside Fog Death Forest, and I don't think we even know the half of what is in there."

"A great place to get a wand then."

"Sabrina's always been an adrenaline junkie," Celeste said, she was sitting on the opposite side of her sister. "Anything for a thrill."

Sabrina rolled her eyes. "Trust me, I don't go to this place unless I have to. To make a Prismatic Wand I need to get Dryad wood, and there's only one place I know where we can find Dryads."

"Dryads?" I asked. "What's that?"

"Tree people," Zelda said from the back of the van. "They're magical creatures—super weird and super dangerous!"

"Great," I muttered under my breath.

"Don't worry, I've dealt with these guys once before," Sabrina said. "We have a pretty good relationship. They gave me the wood for the last wand I made."

"Yeah, and last time we came here we nearly died," Celeste reminded her sister.

"What happened?" I asked. "The Dryads attacked?"

"No, not the Dryads," Sabrina said with a shake of her head. "Hags, we got attacked by hags."

"Excuse me, *hags?* Like... old women?"

"Not women," Celeste corrected. "They only look human, and even then, only barely. They have the vague appearance of an old woman. They're actually creatures, kind of like an ape sort of looks like a human, like that?"

"Hey, we got away okay, didn't we?" Sabrina said.

"Yeah, but Zelda didn't sleep for a month!" Celeste pointed out. I glanced back to see Zelda, who was staring into the distance with a faraway look in her eye.

After twenty minutes of driving Sabrina directed me to a quiet dirt parking lot. We got out of the van and stared at a dark wall of trees ahead of us. An old and slanted wooden sign in the corner of the lot had the words 'Fog Death Forest' written upon it.

"Come on then," Sabrina said after we all took a fearful moment to stare at the dark trees. "Let's get this over with."

As we walked forward and the trees surrounded us things became very quiet. It was almost like sound itself was too scared to venture in here. The trees were unusually dark, the wood almost black in its color. After a few minutes of walking, I noticed a thin carpet of purple mist curling over the ground.

For the most part we walked in silence, which was highly unusual for our group. At least one person was always talking, and usually two people were bickering about something else. I don't know how long we were walking into that deep dark forest, but it had to be at least twenty minutes before Sabrina finally stopped and said something.

"I'm pretty sure it's here, I remember that tree over there, the one that looks like it's got claws."

"They all look like they've got claws," Celeste noted.

Sabrina turned and looked at me. "Can you wake up Hermes? I need him to guide us the rest of the way."

I pulled Hermes out of my bag and placed him on the ground. For a few seconds he was standing up still asleep, but then he opened his eyes. "Ah, in Fog Death Forest again, are we?"

"I think this is the point we stopped at last time. How do we find the Dryads from here?" Sabrina asked.

Hermes looked around in all directions, yawned and pointed to the right. "Pretty sure it's that way."

"Pretty sure, or certain?" Celeste asked. "Because this isn't exactly the type of forest we want to get lost in."

"I'd say 70% sure at least, which is darn sight higher than anyone else here."

And so we ventured off the beaten track, heading deeper into the forest. The ground was thick with wild bracken, and the carpet of mist was growing thicker with every passing minute. All was quiet until another fifteen minutes or so passed—all of a sudden, a colossal and bone-chilling roar echoed through the forest. Strange, winged creatures left the trees around us, and we all froze in terror.

"Uh... what was that?!" Zelda said in horror.

"It was either a Manticore or a Bauk," Hermes said cheerily as he considered the sound. "Either one is bad news!"

"I vote we run," Celeste said quickly. "Now!"

No one else stopped to take that vote, as one we all started sprinting as fast as our feet could go, still heading steadily downhill, vaguely in the direction of the Dryads. Even though it was daytime the leaf canopy overhead was so thick it felt like night in the forest.

"I see something!" Zelda shrieked. I looked over my shoulder and saw something too, a huge gorilla like figure bounding through the mist, a point of light glowing on its forehead.

"Just a little further!" Sabrina shouted. "Don't stop—argh!"

Without warning the ground disappeared underneath our feet and we all hurtled over the edge of a drop. For a second, I wondered if that was the end. Because of the mist I had no idea how long we were going to fall—in reality we hit the ground almost straightaway.

Another colossal roar echoed through the air above us, the sound of stomping feet and crashing trees receding as the thing giving chase gave up its pursuit. We all pushed ourselves to our feet and the mist began to clear. We were in a clearing of trees surrounding a small luminescent lake, its water a brilliant azure blue. A green wall of magical light fenced the clearing off from the rest of the forest, and directly ahead of us I saw a group of unusual trees that looked like they had been sculpted into human figures.

What surprised me further still is that the trees began to move. There were just over a dozen of them in all, they turned and moved forward slowly, the earth around their roots churning as the figures came closer. In a way the Dryads were hauntingly beautiful, with elfin features and sparkling motes of green light hanging around them in the air. Their eyes were bright green, and their bodies were a mixture of humanoid and tree—in some places it was hard to tell where one changed into the other.

They looked like wild angels, carved out of nature itself.

One came forward from the group, a sage darkness etched upon her face. "You come back again," the Dryad said to Sabrina. Her voice was dreamlike and ethereal. "Please explain this unexpected entrance at once."

"We apologize," Sabrina said humbly, lowering her head in respect. "We planned to request entrance politely, but a mysterious creature chased us through the mist."

"The Bauk." The creature nodded in recollection. "It has grown boisterous lately."

"I knew it was a Bauk!" Hermes cheered. We all looked at him reproachfully, silently discouraging any more interruptions. "Uh... sorry," he chuckled nervously.

"So, what brings you here?" the Dryad asked Sabrina.

"This is my cousin, Zora Wick. She's a new witch in Compass Cove, and she's Prismatic."

A look of intrigue came over the Dryad. "Ah yes, we have heard whispers of you on the wind. The witch that solves questions."

"Questions?" I asked.

"Forgive me if my language confuses you—English is not our first tongue. Perhaps there is a better word."

"Mystery," Zelda offered. "She's solved a few mysteries."

"Yes, an excellent way of putting it." The Dryad looked back at Sabrina. "So, what do you need?"

"I need more wood to make a wand. Zelda had to break her other one—it's a long story, but it was necessary."

The Dryad blinked. "I see. Well... we can give you more wood for a wand, but there is something that we need help with first. A small matter. We can make an exchange perhaps?"

"Of course," Sabrina said. "What do you need?"

"Follow me. I will show you."

CHAPTER 5

We followed the dryad down to the small azure pond, the rest of the tree-people gathering around us silently. I couldn't help noticing that we were surrounded on all sides. Sabrina said she trusted these creatures, but it didn't make the current situation any less eerie.

The dryad stopped at the water's edge and turned to face me. "What is your name again, human witch?"

"Zora Wick," I said.

"My name is Glau," the dryad said. "I am the leader of my people. We are small in number, but we work hard to keep control of the darkness in this forest. I guess you could say we are stewards here."

"I see... so what you need from us?"

Glau looked back at the glowing blue pond. "Digby, arise. We have guests."

A transparent blue figure rose out of the water, a mustachioed ghost man wearing the uniform of a union soldier that looked like he was from the 1800s. He was wearing a large, brimmed hat and walked across the water with all the regality of a man from his era.

"Sergeant Digby reporting for duty!" he said, taking his hat off and bowing deeply. The ghost man stood up again and looked upon the group with a courteous smile.

"It's a ghost," I said to the others. Although they'd been charmed to see our Aunt Constance, they couldn't see other ghosts like I could. Hermes of course could see him too.

"Not just any ghost," Glau said as Digby floated over and took her hand. "I believe our souls are destined to be joined as one—the only problem is that we're irrevocably divided."

Digby offered a gentile laugh. "I think what my love is trying to say is that our current physical differences have driven a wedge between our hearts."

"I can see that…" I said, looking at the tree woman and the civil war-era ghost. As far as couples went, they were at the more unusual end of the scale. "What exactly is it I can help you with?"

"There is a ceremony, a way that we can be together as one," Glau said. "We require three items: copper, turquoise, and that which can make one into two. We ask that you acquire these items for us."

"Copper and turquoise I can obtain easily enough—what was that last thing you said?"

"That which can make one into two," Glau repeated.

"Right…" I said after staring at her for a moment.

"What's going on?" Sabrina asked me. I brought the rest of the girls up to speed as I realized they might be a little lost.

"Can you elaborate on this last item?" I asked Glau.

"I find it hard to describe in any other way. It makes one into two, I can't explain it any more clearly."

I looked at Digby's ghost. "Any chance you can help?"

"I'm afraid not," he said with an awkward chuckle. "I've been trying to figure it out for a while now myself. She keeps pointing at the pond—if that is any help."

I looked over at the clear azure water. A gentle curtain of steam wafted up from the surface and the luminescent water projected dancing ripples of light on the tree branches above us. Apart from that I had no idea what Glau meant.

"Anyone here know what she means?" I said, looking at the girls. Everyone shook their heads.

"It's the most important item," Glau explained. "For two to become one, we need one to be two. That is all I can tell you."

"Right… it's just a little vague is all."

"I have faith in you," the dryad said. "You will know it when you see it. Once you return these items to us, you can have more wood for a wand."

"Any chance we could have an upfront payment?" Hermes asked. "Zora kind of blew a hole in the kitchen floor earlier and I'm afraid her current wand is going to cause some real damage soon." The dryad blinked at Hermes, a quiet look of disapproval on her face. "… I'll take that as a no then."

"I'll come with you!" Digby offered. "I'm sure I can help, somehow!"

"Uh, that's okay," I said. I already had enough ghosts following me around.

"No, that's a great idea, darling," Glau said. "I know your heart will recognize the object we need when you see it. Go with the witches. Once you return, we will complete the ceremony and finally be united as one!"

"Then it's settled!" Digby said as he drew a sword from his waist and held it high into the air. "I'll dash any devil that dares to stand in the way of love!"

"I already love this guy," Hermes said with a massive grin on his face.

I really didn't need any more accomplices, but it looked like my mind had been made up for me. "Righto… I guess we'll go and find these items then. Once we have them, we'll come back and get that wood."

Glau nodded. "The deal is made. Please hurry back when you have the three items." The dryad looked at her ghost lover. "My heart will be still until you return!"

"As shall mine, my love! The world already feels bleaker without your presence!"

We began walking back towards the path, scrambling up the sharp descent we had tumbled over only minutes ago.

"Everyone have your wands out this time," Celeste advised. "If we see that creature again, we might have to fight. How long until we get back to the path, Sabrina?"

"If we hurry up, we can be back on the path in fifteen minutes. If we really hurry we can be back to the van in half an hour."

We began the long trek back, and as we walked Digby talked incessantly about his former glory days. I thought Hermes could talk someone's ear off, but Digby made him look like an amateur.

"—then I struck true with my rifle and garroted the so and so! After that I spent six days hiding in a latrine after some Apache Indians teamed up with the South and struck back against our camp, now you might be thinking—Digby, how did you get out of that one—"

"Dude can you just hold off the with the war stories for a minute?" I groaned. "You've been talking non-stop since we left." What made it worse is that the other girls couldn't even hear him.

"Sorry," Digby chuckled. "I thought we should get to know one another if we're going to be spending time together. I can save the stories for later."

"No!" Hermes pleaded. "Zora, come on, this guy is awesome!"

"Well maybe you can arrange a sleepover and do the stories while I'm sleeping, I—"

"Hold on a second," Celeste said, sticking her hand out. She and Sabrina were leading the group as we navigated the dark and quiet forest. They drew back and we all huddled in close.

"What is it?" Sabrina asked.

"There's something out there, two of them. They've been following us for a while now."

"How do you know?" I asked.

"I'm pretty good at Sentio when I want to be," Celeste said. "It's kind of my specialty after cooking."

"Sentio?" I said.

"It's a form of magical meditation," Sabrina said. "You channel all your focus into your senses, and they expand. I'm useless at it."

"Me too," Zelda pipped.

"I'm not that great myself," Celeste said humbly, "but I've been listening and watching ever since we left the dryad camp, someone is following us. I think we need to—" Suddenly Celeste went very quiet and still. Her voice fell to a whisper. "Oh no."

"What? What is it?!" Sabrina said in hushed panic.

"That thing is back," Celeste said, she turned her head slightly to the right and looked off into the trees. "It's coming this way, it's coming quickly!"

"The thing that chased us?!" Zelda shrieked.

"I'll handle this!" Digby said unhelpfully as he produced his ghost sword again.

"Everyone run! Run!" Sabrina shouted.

We raced forward as a group, adrenaline high and breath frantic as we burst through the bracken. Up ahead I heard another colossal roar followed by the sound of crashing trees. It was back.

After a minute of sprinting, we found the path again and skidded on to dirt before running back in the direction of the parking lot. Even at running speed we were at least five minutes away, and something told me the giant figure that had been chasing us could move much faster.

"I see it!" Celeste shrieked. "Oh gosh, it's huge!"

I couldn't help looking back, and as I did, I seriously regretted doing so. About thirty feet behind us a huge beast crashed through the trees, swinging its arms to and frow to clear the path. It looked like a gorilla but four times the size, with huge horns on either side of its head and one white glowing eye.

"Yep, that's a Bauk alright!" Hermes squealed from my bag.

The 'Bauk' opened its jaws to let out another loud roar, its mouth opening wide like a yawning snake. Then without warning it pounced up through the tree canopy and then it was gone. A moment later it crashed back through the canopy fifteen feet ahead of us, its colossal figure landing right in the middle of the path.

As a group we all skidded to a halt at once and screamed. The Bauk opened its mouth and roared again, the deafening sound vibrating through my body and rattling my bones.

"Light!" Hermes shouted. "Light and sound! They hate light and sound!"

In one movement Celeste, Sabrina, and Zelda pulled out their wands and simultaneously uttered incantations for light. The dark path lit up brightly and the Bauk threw its hands over its face and roared again.

"Zora, you too!" Zelda shouted.

I pulled my wand out and stammered a light incantation. "Lux!" In response my wand grew incredibly hot, and a violent ball of wind exploded out from the tip. It was so strong it sent the wands flying out of my friends' hands, and it knocked us all onto our butts. With the wands knocked free the light incantations faded and the Bauk turned its glowing white eye on us again.

With another huge roar it pounded its fists against the ground and sprang forward through the air. We all watched in dismay as the huge beast leapt forward, mere seconds away from crushing us under its huge weight.

Then they came out of nowhere.

Two figures springing from the darkness—a man and a wolf. They burst up and smashed the Bauk in the chest, driving it back in the air and crumbling against the ground. The huge creature sprang onto its feet and started swinging wildly as a chaotic fight broke out between the three. It threw its attackers left and right, but they sprang back, staying close together the entire time.

The fight finally ended with the large wolf snapping at the beast's heals and the man dazing the Bauk with a powerful uppercut. Another roar came from the creature's maw, but this time it was a cry of defeat. Outnumbered and overpowered, it fled into the dark forest, and I knew the fight was over.

Silence followed the battle, my little group watching in stunned amazement at the mysterious shadowy figures on the path ahead.

"That's them!" Celeste whispered. "The ones that have been following us!"

"Who are they?!" Zelda gawped.

The wolf figure shifted into the form of a man and I then heard quiet bickering between the figures on the path.

"Idiot! You call that a joint assault? I could have done that in half the time by myself!"

"Oh, that's rich coming from someone that can't stick to a plan!"

I stood up and helped my friends up too. "I think I have a sneaking suspicion." I walked along the path and as I got closer, I made them both out in the dim light. It was Hudson and Blake. "What in the heck are you guys doing here?" I said to them. They both stopped their fighting and looked at me.

"What's it look like we're doing? Saving your butt, again," Blake said.

Hudson chipped in. "We've been at MAGE trying to get this curse broken. Monty gave me a heads up that you and your friends were heading towards Fog Death Forest. As soon as we got wind of where you went, we decided to come and do our jobs and save your behind. Good thing too by the looks of it."

"Uh we we're doing just fine until Zora's wand malfunctioned," Sabrina pointed out as she and the girls caught up. She handed me the culprit wand.

"Yeah, we were seconds away from scaring that thing away," Celeste said.

"Or seconds away from dying," Zelda added.

"Well look at you two, being forced to work together." As I said this, I realized I had a huge grin on my face. "It's a good look on you both."

"Don't get used to it," Blake grumbled.

"Yeah, as soon as we can lift this curse we're out of here. By the way, what are you doing in here, of all places? Are you out of your minds?" Hudson said.

"I'm trying to get a new wand, which might help with your situation too, so maybe don't be so quick to judge."

"Just give us a heads-up next time you're going to do something stupid," Blake sighed. "I found a grey hair this morning, that can't be a coincidence."

Hudson stared at Blake for a moment. "Hey, I found one too! That only goes to prove it, keeping you out of danger *is* aging me, Zora." Something happened then that had never happened before since the dawn of the universe—Blake and Hudson laughed together.

We all must have been staring in amazement as the boneheaded titans shared their amusement, because they quickly grew serious again. "What's everyone staring at?" Blake said.

"I can't believe it." Zelda blinked as though she was staring at a mirage. "Maw Maw might actually be onto something. It's working, they're getting on!"

"We are *not* getting on," Hudson said quickly, like the idea mightily offended him.

"The idiot is right." Blake yanked a thumb at Hudson. "This is a temporary truce while we're stuck in this situation. No point in killing him if I'll be stuck dragging his corpse around."

"Exactly." Hudson crossed his arms. "I'd have punched his lights out already if I thought it would help."

A new sound disturbed the conversation then, a hair-raising cackle that echoed through the trees.

"Uh, all in favor of running back to the van and getting the heck out of this creepy forest as fast possible?" Celeste said. "Say aye!"

"Aye!" We all said in unison, and we started to run once more.

CHAPTER 6

The trip to Fog Death Forest took much longer than I had anticipated, so when I finally got back to the bakery, I was late for the afternoon bake with Daphne. Normally we only really did our baking first thing in the morning, but it was Patrick Black's party tonight and we were due to bring over the goods that he had paid for.

"Where have you been?!" Daphne said as I came into the kitchen and threw on my apron. "I thought you were going to be back an hour ago!"

"It's a long story, one that involves dryads, a huge demonic beast, and a civil war-era ghost that won't shut up. I'm sorry I'm late. Where are we up to?"

Daphne was red in the face from rushing around the kitchen by herself, she picked up a checklist of jobs from the kitchen counter and handed it to me. "I'm about a third of the way through, if we really hustle, we can get everything baked and decorated before we're supposed to leave for the party."

And so, we hustled. For the next two hours I moved around the kitchen as a blur, Daphne and I working in tandem as we tried our best to get Patrick Black's order done on time. He'd not specifically asked for a list of items, just 'one of everything'—with a lot of the bakes it was easier to make more than one, safer (in case anything messed up), and it looked better presenting multiples, so we had our work cut out for us.

I was actually a little worried we weren't going to get everything done on time because of my tardiness. Obviously, it looked bad from a professional perspective if we didn't deliver something on time. On the one hand I didn't care all that much if we were late delivering Black's order, he was an insufferable jerk and a small part of me reveled in the idea of ruining his night. On the other hand, I knew he'd make my life a living nightmare if we didn't hold up our end of the deal. My driving motivation to get this done was so I could be rid of Black faster.

Somehow, we managed to get everything done in time, and the universe was on my side for once as no distractions came our way during the mad preparation rush. I was decorating a tray of donuts and Daphne was frosting some eclairs as we finally crossed the finish line.

"Done!" she said, panting from being out of breath. She put the eclairs in the fridge and took her apron off.

"Me too." I put my piping bag down on the counter, tapped sprinkles over the last donut and slumped over the table. "I wonder how much of this stuff is actually going to get eaten?"

"Well Ana Akoto is gluten intolerant, and she doesn't look like she's ever eaten a carb," Daphne said. I gave her a look that said *how did you know that?* "What? I'm a big fan."

"I thought Black said his girlfriend was crazy over this stuff?"

"Not his girlfriend *yet*," Daphne emphasized. "And she is crazy for it; she's always posting pictures on the gram with cute bakes. I think she digs the aesthetic more than anything."

"You're telling me we really just busted our butts so a couple of rich weirdos can take some selfies next to cakes? He better be sharing this stuff out; I hate food waste."

"Me too but think of the money!"

"I fall asleep thinking of the money, Daphne. Right, I'm going to go upstairs, shower, and get ready. Meet me back at here at six and then we can run this stuff over to Black's mansion. Sound good?" I asked.

"Sounds good to me chief. I'll meet you back here at six."

Once Daphne left, I put my donuts in the fridge too and headed up to the apartment. I came into the kitchen and found my Aunt Constance and Sergeant Digby floating over the kitchen table.

"Ah, there she is!" Constance said. "Zora, Digby here was just telling me you're helping out the dryads?"

"Trying to. Their shopping list is a little cryptic though."

"I heard, but listen Zora, I think I've cracked it. *That which can make one into two*—it's an axe! An axe cleaves things into two!" Constance held her hands up like I was about to start jumping and celebrating.

"I uh… I don't think it's an axe," I said. "Just call it a hunch."

"Of course it's an axe!" she maintained. "It's a simple riddle, see? That's the answer!"

"Hmm," Digby said from his side of the table. "I'm not so sure madame, you see I know Glau and her people rather well. They are not very fond of axes… for obvious reasons."

"Well why ever not?" Constance stared at him for a moment before realization dawned on her face. "Ah… on account of them being tree people and all."

"It's not a bad guess. Myself I think it's something much more obvious. Every time I asked Glau about it she'd point at the pond. Now what is something that requires water, *and* can make one thing into two?" Digby posited.

"Shark," Hermes said with complete seriousness. I hadn't even realized he was in the kitchen; he was lying on the floor in front of the fridge. There was a little vent there that shot out warm air, so it was one of his favorite nap spots. "Sharks live in water, and they bite people in two. The dryads need a shark to complete their ritual."

Digby looked convinced. "My goodness, it *has* to be a shark!"

Constance didn't look so persuaded. "I think axe is better."

"It's not an axe or a shark," I sighed as I headed off to shower.

"You don't know that for a fact!" Hermes shouted.

"I'd bet my familiar on it," I shouted back.

I shut the bathroom door behind me, turned on the hot water and stared at myself in the mirror for a moment while I waited for the water to heat up. I hadn't realized how filthy I'd got running around the forest. I was caked in dirt from head to toe, my clothes were covered in dust and my hair looked like I'd dragged a hedgehog through it. I was feeling so tired after the day's events that I was half-tempted to drive up to Black's mansion, post his money through the gate and come home for an evening in my pajamas.

Too late now, we've already put the work in.

Besides, the hard part of the job was done now, all we had to do was drive the goods to Black's place, display them in his room and then leave. If we could do all that without seeing him again face-to-face then it would be even easier.

Steam started to fill the bathroom, so I hopped into the shower and scrubbed off the dirt of the day. I had a little time before we had to get out of here, so I spent some time savoring the hot water and enjoying a rare relaxing moment to myself. Once I was clean, I got out, wrapped myself in a huge towel and cleaned my face in the vanity.

Only a few weeks ago I'd seen the reflection of my missing mother in this mirror. After a short period of wondering whether I'd gone crazy or not, we'd learned that my mother had been studying something called the *mirror dimension* just before she vanished. It stood to reason then that I wasn't crazy, and it had *actually* been my mother I'd seen in the mirror. I still had no idea what the meant, or what I was supposed to do about it—but it was the first lead anyone had found in two decades.

The head librarian at Compass Cove Magical Library had said she would help me look into the problem more once I helped *her* out with something—just another item on my long laundry list of chores.

"Zora, Zora!" Constance said as she floated through the bathroom door. I didn't even jump now when she appeared out of nowhere—I was almost desensitized. "What about a zip! A zip makes one into two!"

I put my down my face cream and stared daggers at Constance.

"Remember that talk we had last week about respecting people's privacy?"

"...Yes!" she said after a pause.

"Then you'll remember how I said I want you to stay out of the bathroom while I'm in here."

"Oh, I know, but zip! Zip, Zora! That's got to be it!"

"You think a magical tree person needs a zip so she can be with her ghost boyfriend? Can you hear how crazy that sounds?"

"When you put it that way 'zip' does seem unlikely..."

"Listen Constance, I appreciate you trying to help, but now isn't the time. I've got to get ready, somehow find a smart dress and haul a bunch of cakes and pastries across town for this jackass rock star. Now if you don't mind..."

"Of course, righto Zora. Sorry for the intrusion." Constance floated out of the bathroom, only to pop her head back through the door a second later. I hadn't bothered picking my face cream up again, because I knew she would do this. "Feel free to look in my wardrobe. There's bound to be a smart dress or two in there! The password is 'Bungalow!'"

This time Constance did leave for good.

"What kind of wardrobe has a password?" I muttered to myself.

Once my hair was dry I ventured into Constance's bedroom to see what this wardrobe business was about. I had been in the room once or twice but tried not to come in too often without an invite as Constance usually started throwing things. Her room was odd to say the least, with framed pictures of Donny Osmond covering most of the walls and ceiling.

I walked up to the wardrobe in the corner and had to stifle a scream as a pair of sculpted eyes on the door opened and looked at me. There on the front of the wardrobe was a face... and it started talking.

"Password?" the wardrobe asked. It sounded like a posh old woman from a stately home.

"Uh... Bungalow."

"*Uh... Bungalow* is incorrect."

"Bungalow," I sighed.

"Correct!" the wardrobe sang, its doors opening wide. I stared in bewilderment for a second as I saw a set of stairs going down into darkness. The wardrobe walls and the stairs were covered in patchwork fabric.

"...I just need a smart dress," I said to the wardrobe. "I haven't got time to go to Narnia and fight a war."

"Oh, another Narnia joke, how inspired," the wardrobe said dryly. "I've got a smart dress. What color?"

"I was thinking something olive?"

"Olive? With your skin tone? Darling no. How about... lavender!"

A lavender dress flew up the staircase and hit me in the face. I just about caught it before stumbling back a few paces. "Really?" I said as I thrust the dress down from my face. "No warning?"

"Here's your warning. Don't tumble dry that. Here come the heels!"

This time I just caught the heels before they gave me a pair of black eyes. I grumbled my thanks to the wardrobe before storming back to my room to get dressed. The most annoying thing is that the outfit looked completely killer. "Stupid wardrobe," I muttered while pinning my hair up.

Not long after that Daphne arrived in her own smart dress, a dazzling teal gown with a halter bodice and shimmering chiffon over the top. Black's assistant requested that we wore the elegant party dresses, but made sure to remind us that we weren't allowed at the actual party.

We very carefully loaded our boxes of cakes and pastries into the back of the van, plugged Black's address into my phone and drove across town and up into the hills. Several large mansions sat atop the hill which overlooked the lake and the town, and Black's was right at the end of the street. Large gates separated his property from the road, beyond which there was an expansive driveway and lawns that were all perfectly manicured.

There were expensive looking cars everywhere, and the large mansion was bustling with activity as Black's party was well underway. We pulled up to a security booth at the gate and gave our names. The guard told us to drive around the back of the mansion and park there with the rest of the 'staff'.

"Ugh, *staff*," I said to myself as we drove on through. "I really don't like the idea of being considered one of his workers."

"Oh-em-gee, I think I just saw Nicolas Cage!" Daphne squealed. "There are going to be loads of a-list people here, right?"

"Probably, and we're not meant to be seen by any of them. We get shuttled in through the service doors, drop the goods off and get out of here." I parked up the van in the small lot behind the mansion. Two bodyguards were standing outside an open door, along with a woman who I'd seen in the bakery earlier this week. "That's his assistant, the one that put your photo in the paper. I'm guessing she knows where we have to go. I should really give her a piece of my mind!"

"It's fine, really!" Daphne said in her cheery way. "Honestly, I'm just excited to be at this celebrity party. Don't you think it's exciting?"

"Nope. You start unloading the stuff, I'll see where it's supposed to go." I got out of the van and walked up to the door. As I did Black's assistant looked up from her phone.

"Ah, the bakery woman. I'm Francesca, I met you briefly the other day. I was starting to think you might be late. You better hurry up and bring that upstairs quickly, Akoto is going to be here soon, and Black will throw a fit if everything isn't perfect."

"And we wouldn't want that, would we," I said through gritted teeth.

"I'm glad you understand. Follow me, I'll show you where the room is. After that I want you to take the goods upstairs, and you can consider your part of the job done. No hanging around after that."

I snapped my fingers. "Shucks, and here I was looking forward to rubbing shoulders with the Hollywood elite."

Daphne came over holding two boxes of our goods. I took one off her and we followed Francesca upstairs and into Black's master bedroom. The room itself was bigger than my entire apartment, and the man of the hour was there, playing videogames on a large television.

"It's about time!" he said, taking his eyes off the TV a moment as we came in. "Cutting it close, don't you think?!"

"Shouldn't you be downstairs enjoying your party?" I asked.

"You think I care about those losers? This is all for Ana. Now set the stuff up and get out!"

"Where do you want 'the stuff?'" I asked.

"Set it up on the table, and make it look good!" Black threw his controller down, turned the tv off and walked across the master bedroom to a small kitchenette area to make himself a drink. "Hey, you there, cheekbones," he said to Daphne. "No hard feelings about that story the other day, right?"

"Oh, none at all!" Daphne said nervously as she placed her box down on a long table at the back of the room.

Black pulled the stopper from a bottle of whiskey and held it up to me in mock salute. "See? She's fine. Now go and bring up the rest of your crap. I want you out of here before Ana arrives!"

We followed Francesca back downstairs to the service entrance. "Take the goods up and then make yourself scarce," she reminded us. "I have to go and check on the party. Leroy and Mike here will be watching you. *Don't* try to sneak in after you're finished."

"No danger of that, *really*," I stressed.

We walked back to the van and started unloading things properly. There was a little folding trolley in the van for moving boxes. I hadn't used it before but figured it would come in handy for cutting down the number of trips we had to make back and forth. There were about thirty boxes in all. While I struggled with the trolley, Daphne took another armful of boxes. "I'll run these up while you get that thing sorted."

"Alright!" I huffed while trying to kick a folding arm on the trolley open. There was a chance Constance had never used this thing, so it was a little stiff. After struggling for another minute, I gave up on the trolley, grabbed some boxes myself and hurried upstairs to catch up with Daphne—it wasn't fair to let her do all of this by herself.

I had just finished climbing the stairs and turned onto the corridor for the master bedroom when a scream cut through the air. Quickening my pace, I walked through the open doors and then I saw him lying in the middle of the room.

Patrick Black's throat was cut open and there was blood everywhere, his lifeless eyes staring at the ceiling. Daphne was crouched over and holding him, blood all over her dazzling teal dress. She took one look at me, her face white as a sheet.

"Zora!" she gasped. Daphne looked down at her dress and realized she was covered in blood too. "It's... it's not what it looks like! It wasn't me!"

CHAPTER 7

I almost couldn't believe this was happening all over again. Only a few weeks ago I'd stumbled upon my first ever dead body, and now here I was again watching in shock as my friend clutched the dead body of one of the most famous rock stars in the world.

"I came into the room, and he was lying on the floor!" Daphne said. "I swear!"

"What is all the racket about?!" Francesca said as she came into the room. As she saw Patrick Black on the floor she screamed too. "He's dead! Dead! She killed him!"

"I was trying to help him!" Daphne protested. She let go of Black and stumbled back, staring at her hands.

"Security, security!" Francesca screamed.

"Let's all just take it easy. Someone needs to call the police."

Take it easy they did not. It wasn't long before every Tom, Dick, and Harry had rushed to the landing outside Patrick Black's master bedroom. Word quickly spread throughout the house and half a dozen of Black's huge security guards pushed into the room and stared in disbelief at their boss lay dead on the floor.

"Make sure she doesn't go anywhere!" one of the guards shouted to another. He pointed a finger at Daphne, who was still sitting on the floor in the middle of the bedroom, her face whiter than a pail of milk.

"Get these people back downstairs," I said to one of the guards as I looked over at the crowd of people trying to eyeball the crime scene. "Make sure no one leaves the house."

"Yeah? And who are you to give orders? I'm in charge here, I say what happens."

"Great, then you'll agree that my plan is the best course of action."

"Maybe. Personally I'm going to make sure no one leaves, *then* I'll tell them to get downstairs," the huge guard said.

"That's exactly the same as my plan but just the other way around."

"Right!" the guard said, turning his attention to the crowd on the landing. "Everyone get downstairs! No one is to leave until the police say so!"

"This is unbelievable," Francesca said as a quiet returned to the scene. "I mean I know you probably weren't happy about the story in the paper, but killing a man? A man like Patrick Black as well?"

"She said she didn't kill him," I said to the irate assistant. "So, she didn't kill him."

Francesca threw her hands up and blew air out of her lips. "Oh well I guess we'll just let her go then! The woman covered in blood! The woman who was found crouched over the dead body!"

"You need to take a couple of steps back and get out of this room," I said calmly. "This reaction isn't helping anyone."

"Oh, I'm not going anywhere. I'm staying until the police turn up and arrest you both. Probably figures that you're in this together!"

It was only five minutes until the police did arrive, but what an agonizing five minutes that was. Blake walked through the door, closely accompanied by Hudson. I should have figured they'd be together seeing as they couldn't physically be further than ten feet apart.

"There she is officers!" Francesca shouted as they walked in. "She's the one that killed him, and that there is her accomplice!"

Blake and Hudson both took one look at the crime scene and then looked at me.

"Are you cursed or something?" Blake said in exasperation.

"Seriously…" Hudson added. "How does this keep happening to you?"

"Does either of you think I enjoy this?" I asked. "It just happens!"

"First, we save you back in the forest…" Hudson said.

"And now this!" Blake added. They both looked at one another and shook their heads in disbelief. If it was any other moment, I'd be delighted to see them getting on, but I really didn't need them teaming up to make fun of me right now.

"Excuse me? What is going on here?" Francesca said. "Do you know this woman?! This accomplice to a murderer!"

Blake rolled his eyes and looked at Francesca. "My name is Officer Voss. This here is my associate… Hudson…" He paused and glanced over. "What is your last name anyway?"

"Beck," Hudson said. "My family comes from Germany originally."

Blake's eyes lit up. "My family came from Germany too! My grandmother used to make the most amazing bratwurst—"

"Bratwurst! Now there's a taste of home I haven't had in a while, I tell you, I love nothing better than some real mustard, some brat—"

I cleared my throat to interrupt them. "Look I love that you guys are getting on now, but can you pick literally any other time to have your Brokeback moment?" I said. They both looked at me, Blake looked back at Francesca.

"Uh, where was I? Oh yes. I'm Officer Voss. This is my associate, Mr. Beck."

"I don't care!" Francesca said. "You have to arrest these women now! They killed Patrick Black!"

"Zora Wick has helped Compass Cove Police Station solve several murder cold cases recently, I can assure you she didn't kill anyone," Blake said dismissively.

"Well, she did!" Francesca shrieked, pointing her finger at Daphne. "Look at her! She's covered in blood!"

"I was just trying to help him," Daphne said in her defense.

"Let's calm down here," Blake said. "What's your name?"

"Francesca, Francesca Stanley. I'm Mr. Black's assistant!"

"Okay Francesca, I'd like you to go downstairs with my associate here and—"

"How is that going to happen?" Hudson interrupted.

Blake looked at him. "What?"

"How am I going downstairs. Where are you going to be?"

"I'll stay up here and—" He paused as he realized the flaw in his plan. They were still joined together with Nana Bucktooth's curse. "Oh, for the love of... right. Okay, I'm going to have to call for Burt and the boys to come down for backup." Blake pulled out his phone and made the call.

While Blake was on the phone Hudson eyed up the large security guards dotted around the room. "Who's in charge of security?" he asked.

"Me," one of the men said, standing up from the couch. "Name's Axel."

"Alright Axel, could you do me a favor and take your men downstairs? Make sure no one leaves the house, we need to question everyone before we leave here. We'll hold the fort up here. Take her too." Hudson nodded at Francesca. "Officer Voss and I will interrogate the suspects in private."

"Got it," the large security guard said. He had a much easier time taking instructions from Hudson than he did from me apparently.

Once the security guards left the air in the room felt lighter, despite the fact we were all standing several feet away from a dead body. "So we're 'suspects' now?" I said to Hudson.

"Just getting them out of here. Obviously, we don't think you did it." He took a look at Daphne and paused. "You have to admit this doesn't look good though. Can you talk me through what happened?"

We recalled our brief arrival at the mansion, and the two trips made up to the room. Blake—who had finished on the phone—and Hudson listened carefully. "I came back into the room the second time and there he was on the floor!" Daphne recalled. "I ran over to see if I could help him... I wasn't even thinking."

"You did the right thing," Blake said. "How long were you both downstairs before you came back up again?"

"It was probably about ten minutes," I said. "It's quite a big house. Walking to the van from here is probably three minutes in itself. Coming back with boxes is another four or five. We were trying to get a trolley to unfold too, but it was stuck."

Both Blake and Hudson gazed around the room. "So, let's be generous and say the killer had ten minutes," Hudson said. "Where do you think they went?"

Together he and Blake tentatively walked forward into the room. I imagined it was difficult being magically joined to another person, but it looked like they'd already got the hang of the curse, mostly. At one point Hudson went to walk into the kitchen, causing the spell to pull Blake back with him.

"Watch it!" Blake growled.

"Don't get your panties in a twist, it was a mistake!" Hudson fired back.

I couldn't help smiling. Even if they were getting on better, they still had that animosity. "What are you guys doing?" I asked.

"Seeing if the killer might be hiding anywhere in the room. The windows are all closed so they didn't leave that way…" Blake looked up at the ceiling as if there was some magic hatch for the killer to leave through.

"Hello!" Hudson said. "I think I've found the murder weapon. Here in the sink!"

Blake and I went over to the sink which was empty apart from one thing—a square piece of shiny metal covered in blood. "What is that thing?" Blake said as he leaned into get a better look.

"It's a bench scraper," I said. "We usually use them when kneading and chopping dough."

They both looked at me. "This is *your* bench scraper?"

My forehead creased. "What? No. I said *a* bench scraper. Not ours. We did all our baking back the shop. We didn't bring any tools with us."

"Doesn't look good for this to be here," Hudson mumbled, "even if it isn't yours."

"It *isn't* ours!" I repeated.

He held his hands up. "I believe you! I'm just saying, given that girl is already screaming about you both being the killers, a bench scraper being the murder weapon doesn't look good!"

"Well…" Darn it. He did have a point.

"Looks like Billy Idol here had one last smoke before he got his throat slit," Blake said, nodding at a cup on the counter. He held it up, revealing a still-smoking cigarette inside.

"That can't be right," Daphne said. "Patrick Black didn't smoke. I've read it in like a million interviews. His mom died of lung cancer."

Hudson and Blake looked at one another. "Left behind by the killer possibly?" Hudson posited.

"Definitely possible," Blake said with a nod.

Axel, the large security guard came back to the room a few minutes after that. "More police have just pulled up outside. People are starting to ask a lot of questions downstairs, they want to know if they can leave."

"Not until we say so," Blake said as he looked across the room. "What are you doing over there Zora?" he asked.

There was a large bookshelf running across the back wall of the master bedroom, and I was currently standing in front of it, my eyes wandering over the shelves. "I'm wondering if Patrick Black was a reader—this bookcase certainly suggests so."

"Just a decorative element," Axel contributed from the door. I turned to regard him. "He never read."

"Still… looks like someone checked the books out recently," I said, nodding at a gap on the shelf. The gap in itself wasn't evidence, but there was a red smudge on the white shelf, glistening and still wet. Blake and Hudson came over to look at it.

"Blood!" Hudson remarked.

"The killer took a book…" Blake deduced. "Good find Zora!"

I turned and looked at the security guard again. "Who would want Black dead?"

"Seems like that question is already answered," he said, nodding over at Daphne.

"Not her you donkey-brain moron," I snapped. "She's innocent! Who knew Black the best? Who could help us with these answers?"

"Well, I worked for him for quite some time," Axel said defensively. "I figure I know a thing or two about him. Heck, as security I'd say we're probably the leading authority. It was our job to assess and detain threats."

"Any that jump to mind straightaway?" Hudson asked.

The large man thought about it a moment, the gears in his brain turning at a snail's pace. Then a look of recognition came over his eyes. "Actually yeah, now you mention it. We had to fire one of our own recently, Jack, Jack Lawson."

"What happened?" Blake said.

"Jack was a good guy," Axel said, "But Black slept with his wife one night after a gig. Lawson nearly ripped Black's head off when he found out. Took six of us to drag him off him."

"When was this?" I asked.

"A few months back."

"Doesn't seem likely he's the murderer," Hudson pointed out. "He wasn't here tonight, was he?"

Axel shook his head. "That's the thing, one of my men picked him up earlier. He was trying to sneak in. We stopped him and turned him around. He knew the house well though, wouldn't have been hard for him to find another way in."

Blake, Hudson and I all gave each other the look. This spurned employee had definitely just moved onto the suspect list.

"Anyone else you can think of?" I asked.

"I'll be honest, he had more than his share of enemies. I could write some names down for you. Might be worth speaking with Francesca too—she knew Patrick better than most."

"We need to look around and see if that guy snuck in or not," I said to Blake and Hudson. "He's definitely a person of interest."

"Agreed," Hudson said.

Just then Sheriff Burt walked into the master bedroom with the town coroner, Tamara Banana. Tamara was also the town's only crime scene investigator. "Yikes," she said as she pulled on a pair of blue gloves and headed over to the body. "Let's see what we have here then."

Burt remained near the door. Although he wore the sheriff badge he treated the role casually—Blake, Hudson, and I were the ones that did the majority of the investigating.

"What have we got here then?" he said as he looked across the room. "A dead rock star?" His gaze fell on Daphne. "Why'd you do it, girl?"

"I didn't do it! I tried to help him!"

"She's innocent," I said to Burt. "Daphne didn't hurt him."

An unsure look came over Burt's face. "Well, if the woman covered in blood didn't do it, who did?" He looked at the three of us. "Any leads?"

"One so far," Blake answered. "We still need to sweep through the party and talk to everyone that was here."

Burt nodded as though he approved. "Good, good. Well, we best get on it then. Wayne and Zayne are downstairs. Wick, what's your take on this?"

"Just a girl in the wrong place at the wrong time… again." I sighed.

He chuckled. "I'll say. Obviously, I want you on this one again. Had a word with this big boss upstate and we've found a little room in the budget to officially take on hired help. We'll even cut you a check this time!"

"Uh, great, thanks," I said tonelessly.

"It's not all good news though," Burt's gaze fell on Daphne again. "Voss you're going to have to arrest this woman."

Blake's face fell. "But chief, she's—"

"You can't!" I shouted. "She's innocent, she didn't do anything!"

Burt held out his hands. "Look I believe you, and believe me missy, I think you most likely *are* innocent. But you have to understand how this looks from a public perspective. What would people say if police turned up and didn't arrest the woman found covered in blood over the body? My hands are bound on this one Wick. We can only hold her for so long anyway, but it's a formality. You have to understand."

"Sheriff, I—" Blake began.

"I won't hear another word against it. Handcuff this woman and take her to the car. I'll head downstairs and help the boys question folks." Burt looked at me. "Zora Wick, if you want to help clear your friend's name then you best start putting that magic of yours to work."

"Magic?" I gulped. Burt was a human, and as such he wasn't supposed to know I was a witch. As far as I knew he didn't know.

"Yes, that mystery solving ability of yours! Get to work!"

Burt left the room. Blake regretfully handcuffed a shocked Daphne and led her outside, Hudson following closely behind. I looked at the lead security guard and sighed.

"I'm going to need that list of names. Pronto."

CHAPTER 8

"Hm, interesting," Tamara Banana said as she took a closer look at the body. Since arriving she'd gone back to her car and returned with her suitcases full of mobile lab equipment. She was currently crouched over Patrick Black's body with a magnifying glass. We were the only ones in the room at the moment.

"What is it?" I asked.

"Whoever cut this guy knew what they were doing. They went straight for the carotid artery, it's a very neat cut as well, almost looks surgical. Do we have a murder weapon yet?" Tamara lifted her head and looked at me, her eyes magnified behind several layers of lenses. She flicked the lenses up.

"Hudson found a bloodied bench scraper in the kitchen sink," I said. Tamara went over to the sink and picked up the scraper, holding it between her fingers as she turned it around and inspected it in the light.

"People use these in kitchens, right? Is it one of yours?"

"No," I said with a sigh. "Though I realize it doesn't look good it being here."

"I wouldn't have thought these things would be sharp enough to slice a man's neck, but…" She turned it over, so the edge was facing the light. "This one certainly seems sharp enough."

"Yeah, some of them have a pretty thin edge. I've nipped my finger on them before."

Tamara slipped the scraper into a Ziplock evidence bag and sealed it. "Okie doke. Well I better get this body bagged and put on ice. I can do a more thorough examination back at the morgue. As for the rest of the scene I've not noticed anything new. I think you guys spotted it all. I've bagged up the cigarette found in the cup and taken a photograph of the bloody smudge on the shelf. Can you find Blake and ask him to come back up here? I'll need a hand moving the body onto a gurney."

"Aye, aye, captain." I saluted and made my way out of the room. The hallway outside the master bedroom branched right and left. Heading right lead to the stairs which Daphne and I had used to bring up the cakes and pastries. I followed the corridor to the left and found a large staircase that descended into a huge entrance hall. I went down the stairs and found Wayne Combs at the bottom, one of Sheriff Burt's sons.

"Seen Blake anywhere?" I asked him.

"In the kitchen, he's talking with Black's assistant. It's through that door just there."

I thanked Wayne and went through the door to find a kitchen that was easily twice the size of my entire apartment. Blake and Hudson were in there along with Francesca, the assistant from upstairs. She was teary eyed now, dabbing her face with a tissue.

"Tamara needs a hand upstairs with the body," I said to Blake. "It needs to go on ice."

Blake nodded. "Alright, I was just talking with Francesca here, maybe you could take over. I'll go upstairs and help with the body, Hudson you stay here and—" Hudson gave Blake a look and he caught his mistake again. "Actually, come upstairs with me, I need some help. I threw my back out… doing something."

"Good cover," Hudson said and rolled his eyes. The two of them went upstairs and I took a seat across from Francesca.

"I'm sorry," she said to me. "I shouldn't have accused you upstairs, it was a little overwhelming in the moment. That officer says you've solved a few mysteries here?"

"Yeah, I've got a talent for tripping over this stuff. I know how it looked, but I promise you my friend Daphne didn't do it either—I don't know what happened, but I *will* get to the bottom of it."

Francesca pressed the already wet tissue against her eyes and took a very deep breath to steady herself. Her whole face was red and blotchy. "The shock and the emotions are catching up with me now."

"That's entirely normal. I spoke with Patrick's head of security upstairs, Axel, he said there was an ex-security staff member that we should talk to, a Mr. Jack Lawson. Have you seen him at the party tonight?"

Francesca shook her head. "No, he was fired months ago. He wasn't on the list."

"Axel said he was caught trying to sneak in though."

She looked taken aback by this news. "First I've heard of it. Still, I didn't see him—I would remember if I had."

"Alright. Is there anyone else you can think of that might have had reason to hurt Patrick? Enemies? People he wronged?"

Francesca laughed slightly. "I mean you only knew him briefly, but you saw what he was like. Patrick did what he wanted; he made no secret of his opinions either. He… rubbed a lot of people the wrong way."

"Any names that jump to mind straightaway?" I asked.

"Where do I even begin," she said in a dazed manner. Francesca pulled out a smartphone and started swiping through some sort of long list. "This is all of the people that were invited to the party tonight. Patrick calls them his friends, but I'd say at least a third of them hate his guts. A lot of my job is making sure that Patrick doesn't know what people really think about him."

"That's a lot of names," I said as I watched her scroll through the list. "Is there anyone that you instantly suspect though, other than this rogue security guard?"

Francesca thought about it for a moment and then nodded to

herself. "For the longest time I've thought that Molly was going to do something. I mean... things got really crazy with them for a while."

"Molly?" I asked.

"Molly Gould?" she said as though it made things any clearer.

"I don't really keep up with pop culture."

"I see. Well Molly is... hm, how do I put this? She says she's a popstar, but she's mostly famous for her online entertainment, if you know what I mean."

"She's a vlogger."

"Uh, *kind of*. One that makes a lot of money by not wearing very many clothes."

"Ah, I think I get you. So, what was her relationship with Black?"

"They dated, and they were engaged to be married. Molly actually loved him, or that's what I believed at least. They were good together, and she really tamed that wild side of Patrick. I actually thought he'd settle down and become an honest man, but..."

"But that didn't happen, he ditched her?"

"He didn't just ditch her, he almost ruined that girl. Patrick had a bunch of stories put on the web saying how she'd cheated on him and broken his heart. In actual fact he'd been cheating on her. If there's one thing you have to understand about Patrick it's that his fans are psychotic, they made Molly's life a living hell."

"Isn't it your job to put those stories in the papers?" I said, recalling how Francesca had done the same to Daphne.

"I'm no saint, but I had nothing to do with the smear campaign Patrick set up against Molly. She was actually a pretty good friend of mine before their relationship went south. Patrick went behind my back and used an outside public relations firm. He was a snake like that sometimes." Francesca took a sip of water and let out another calming breath.

"And Molly was here tonight?" I asked.

She nodded. "Yup, and out of all the guests I have her down as most likely to kill him. Whether or not she did though... well I guess that's for you to find out."

"I'll definitely make sure to talk to her then. Is there anyone else you think it might be worth talking with—"

"Wick just what in the tarnation do you think you're doing?" Sheriff Burt asked as he walked into the kitchen.

"I'm uh... working the case, just like you asked me to."

Burt walked forward and laughed awkwardly, scratching a hand over the back of his head. "Well that's true, I guess I did ask you to work the case—but now that I think about it that was a mighty stupid decision for me to make. Blake probably introduced you to Hudson, the guy that's been following him around like a lost puppy dog."

"Hudson? I already know him. He was a suspect in the Marjorie Slade case, I helped clear his name and he saved my life."

Burt stared at me for a moment like this was all news to him. "Right, right. Of course. I remember that. *Vividly*. Anyway, Blake's got Hudson helping him out now, so your assistance won't be required on this case. You can head on out—this is an active crime scene after all."

I looked back at Burt in confusion, wondering where this change of heart had come from. "All the times I've helped you guys out and this is when you close the door? Daphne is my friend, and she's innocent! I'm not going to let her go down for this! You have to let me... oh," I said, drawing the word out over a very long syllable. I realized what was going on now.

"What's happening here?" A confused Francesca asked, looking between us both.

"You think I'm going to be biased," I said to Burt.

He smiled awkwardly and scratched his head some more. "I didn't want to come out and say it in so many words, Wick, but you've cut to the crux of the matter. I'm afraid you can't work this one. Now if you would so kindly pack up your things..."

And just like that I was off the case. I had faith that Blake and Hudson were capable of solving this by themselves, but it still didn't change the fact that Daphne had been led away in handcuffs and was currently on her way to a jail cell.

I just had to hope the guys could solve this thing without me.

***

It had been a pretty stressful day and I expected the day's events to effect my sleep—to my surprise I fell asleep pretty much the moment my head the pillow that night, but little did I know there were other things brewing.

I dreamed frequently and often, I even made an effort to try and record my dreams whenever I woke up. I found that it was easier for me to recall dreams after I made a frequent habit of writing them down, so I tried to do it every morning.

At some point I found myself floating through dreams—I was in the bakery working the register, and there were hundreds of people crammed into the shop. Zelda, Daphne and I were all running around like headless chickens as we tried to keep up with the demand.

"Don't worry!" Sabrina said as she punched through the wall. "Celeste and I are here to help!"

"Brilliant!" I replied, not even batting an eye at their unusual entrance. "Grab an apron and start serving!"

I didn't yet realize that I was dreaming, but I suddenly found myself becoming lucid when the dream froze. It was like someone had hit pause, the bustling crowd of customers and even the girls working behind the register with me all stopped. For a second it was eerily quiet, and then the front door opened.

"Too busy here!" the voice of an old woman said. I couldn't see who it was because of the crowd, but I saw a wrinkled old hand lift into the air and snap its fingers. All of the frozen customers in the shop shattered, crumbling to the floor like broken stone.

"What the…" I muttered, watching as my cousins crumbled around me as well. Looking forward I saw Nana Bucktooth walk towards the counter, scowling in disapproval as she took in the bakery.

"I never liked what Constance did with this place, I preferred it when old Herbert had his medicine shop here. Sold morphine out the bottle, $1 for two!" the old woman walked up to the counter and slapped her hand down. "Still, I guess the kids of today can't live without their sugar…"

"Is this a dream?" I said, looking at my own hands as if it would make things clearer.

"You're dreaming alright, missy, but this conversation is *very* real."

"You're invading my dreams now?" I asked. I didn't understand how, but I knew that despite this being a dream this was the real Nana Bucktooth visiting me in my sleep.

"It's called dream craft, never heard of it? I don't know why I'm asking, you're so wet behind the ears you could hide the Titanic back there. Mind you I never liked the film, they got it all wrong. The ship was pretty accurate of course, but the passengers were nothing like that. I was there, I should know!" Nana Bucktooth jabbed a bony finger in my direction.

"*You* were on the Titanic?" I said in disbelief.

"Yeah, I was. Stole a ticket off this snotty middle-class girl when I worked as a dancer in Southampton. I was kind of like that boy the girl-faced man played in the movie?"

"Leonardo DiCaprio?"

"Yeah, that sissy! I met a man in upper class and boy did he take a liking to me. I milked that boy dry. We did it in the cabin, did it on the deck after dark, we even did it in the—"

"I *really* don't need to hear this," I said, having to look away from the old woman so my mind didn't start running away from me.

"Stop being so precious, it's just sex! Besides my body looked a lot better back then. None of this sagging skin, I was tighter than a—"

"Yeah, I'm gonna cut that story short there," I said. "And I'm assuming it *is* just a story, because if you were really on the Titanic you'd be well over a hundred years old."

"Well look at that, the idiot can do math! I'll have you know I just celebrated my 128th birthday, not that I look a day over one hundred."

I just stared at the old witch. Obviously, she liked to tell tall tales. "Okay, sure. You're super old. I believe you."

"Like I care if you believe me or not? You can go and look at my birth certificate in the town records for all I care. Let's get to business anyway, I don't want to waste all night talking to you! I came here for a reason!"

"And why's that?" I asked.

"I'm still waiting on your visit," Bucktooth said. "And believe me girl, I don't like being made to wait. Now when the sun comes up tomorrow you and Zelda are going to get your butts down here, no excuses! I don't want to have to throw a curse on you as well."

I gulped, recalling how Nana Bucktooth had ruined Hudson and Blake's lives with a snap of her fingers. "That won't be necessary. I can visit briefly, but I don't have anyone to run my shop now. My assistant was arrested yesterday on suspicion of murder."

An unusual grin spread over the old woman's face. "So, some of your girls do have stones! It's refreshing to hear! Don't worry about your shop, I know a good girl that can take care of it. She's an extremely competent baker and she's the only other woman that I'm afraid of! I'll send her over tomorrow morning!"

"That uh… won't be necessary," I said, wondering what kind of psychopath this old woman would be afraid of. "I'll just close for the morning."

"Nonsense! We can't have you losing out on custom. We witches have to stick together! I'll go and pay her a visit now and tell her to be up early tomorrow morning. I won't hear another word!"

I went to open my mouth to argue the point further, but she snapped her fingers and my jaw clamped shut. I couldn't open my lips even an inch. With another snap of her fingers the old woman vanished, and the dream around me crumbled into darkness until it was gone.

With a start I woke in my bed, I sat bolt upright, my breath racing and my skin covered in sweat.

Even sleep wasn't sacred now.

CHAPTER 9

I must have fallen back asleep at some point, because I didn't wake up again until nine.

"Sleeping in today?" asked Hermes, he was sitting on top of me and staring at me.

"You are without doubt the creepiest cat I know," I said as I pushed him off.

"I'll take that as a compliment. Don't you have to do the morning bake?"

"No, we're closed for the morning. Nana Bucktooth visited me in my dreams last night and told me to hurry my butt over to Wildwood if I want to see out the rest of the week without being cursed. I woke up in the middle of the night covered in sweat. Figured I might as well turn off the early alarm and get a good night's sleep."

Hermes cackled. "That old crone is visiting you in your dreams now? She must really need your help."

"How does a witch do that?" I asked. "She said it was something called dream craft?"

He nodded. "Yeah, it's very advanced divination magic. I have no idea how she does it to be honest."

"So Bucktooth is a Divination witch," I said... "I'll make a note of that. It'll be handy to know." I swung my legs out of bed and started getting ready for the day.

"Uh no, she doesn't really pay attention to any of that stuff. Bucktooth does her own thing."

"What do you mean? I thought all witches fell into the main magical types?"

"*Most* do. Witches that pay attention to the magical types tend to be more powerful, that's why so many ascribe to it. Then there are wild witches like Bucktooth that do their own thing. She's a proponent of wild magic—she just goes by instinct, and she's very good at it too. I reckon she's even more powerful than Liza."

Liza was my grandmother, who also lived here in Compass Cove. She lived over on the east coast of the lake, in the town of Eureka. She was somewhat of a recluse, and I'd only seen her a handful of times since moving here. Apparently, she was busy with her own work, but what that was I didn't actually know.

I made my way into the kitchen and made some coffee and a quick breakfast. I'd only been up for five minutes when there was a knock on my door. I opened it and wasn't surprised to see Zelda, dressed and ready to go.

"Come on, she's waiting, we have to hurry up!" she said in a panic as she came inside.

"I'm guessing you got a dream visit too." I sat down at the kitchen table and took a bite out of my bagel.

"Yes, and she only resorts to infiltrating dreams when she's serious, so we should hurry up and get over there!"

"I'm sure the old crone can wait while I finish my breakfast. What were you dreaming about when she came to you?"

"I uh… don't remember," Zelda said guardedly. My sister wasn't a great liar at the best of times, and obviously was embarrassed by whatever she had been dreaming about.

"Ha, if you say so. I was having some weird anxiety dream about the bakery being super busy. She came in, snapped her fingers and everyone crumbled around me like stone."

Zelda laughed awkwardly and joined me at the table. "Yeah, she can be pretty terrifying when she wants to be. I had to message Celeste and tell her I wasn't going to be in this morning. She was pretty unhappy until I told her Maw Maw had requested my help."

"So everyone is scared of Bucktooth then?" I asked Zelda.

She nodded. "Oh definitely. I mean she's highly respected, and most of the time she's quite reasonable... even if she comes across differently. A lot of people around here owe a lot to Nana Bucktooth, she's a pillar of the community."

"A shotgun wielding, eyepatch wearing pillar that invades peoples dreams, kicks down doors and scares the life out of everyone."

"She's not without her quirks, that's for sure."

After I finished my hurried breakfast, I went and got dressed quickly. Zelda and I were just about to leave when the buzzer went. I leaned in and pressed the button. "Hello?"

A strong Irish accent came back. "It's Rosie, give me a hand with this stuff, it's heavier than it looks!"

"Rosie?" I asked, looking back at Zelda. She just shrugged at me. We headed downstairs and outside the back door we found a small redhead woman with two huge boxes in her arms.

"Here!" she said and dumped one in mine and Zelda's arms. "Take them in, I'll get the rest!"

Before we could question things, the small woman disappeared around the corner. Zelda and I looked at one another in bewilderment.

"You hired someone new?" she asked.

"No, but Nana Bucktooth did say she'd send someone around to cover the bakery this morning..."

Just then the stranger came back around the corner carrying more boxes. "Well go on!" she shouted. "Get inside and let me past!"

We took the boxes inside and set them down in the kitchen. 'Rosie' came in behind us and set her stuff down too. "Forgive the question, but who are you, and what's in the boxes?" I asked.

"Rosie," she said, holding her hand out to shake mine. Her vice-like grip left me holding my hand. "Boxes are full of bakes, made fresh this morning. I've been up since three getting it altogether. Bucktooth said you needed help."

"But I... I—" I watched in amazement as Rosie opened up one of the boxes. There were all sorts of see-through containers with elaborate-looking pastries and cakes inside. "My goodness, this stuff looks delicious!"

"Tastes even better than it looks too," she said as she carried on unpacking. "Here, try a danish."

Rosie threw a pastry my way and I caught it. She launched one at Zelda too, but she didn't react as fast, and it smacked her in the face.

I took a bite and sure enough it was top drawer. "Okay, consider me impressed. Who are you again?"

"Just a girl that knows her way around the kitchen. Now don't you worry about the bakery, I'll take care of everything while you're gone. I've worked a register before, and I know how to upsell too. I will warn you that I won't take any nonsense from customers. Full disclosure, I got fired from my last job because a customer got handsy and I used my magic to throw him through a window. Got my wand taken away as well for three months."

Zelda and I exchanged a nervous look. "Uh..." I began.

"But don't you worry about that! I've got things under control now since I was inside. They have a real good shrink inside the local county jail."

"Right," I said slowly, not sure how to turn this woman away even if I wanted to. "It all sounds..." It sounded like Rosie was a loose cannon. "The bakes look great."

"They put you in jail for throwing a guy through a window?" Zelda asked.

"No, the woman that responded to that said I was somewhat justified seeing as he harassed me and all—still took my wand away though. The jailtime was for blowing up my ex's truck—but in my defense it was payback for him sleeping with that girl! Judge said it was the third strike so I was out, would you believe that?" *Third strike?* "Anyway, don't let me keep you gals, I know Bucktooth doesn't like being made to wait. You can rest safe knowing your shop is in good hands, Zora. Y'all have a good morning now!"

Rosie practically ushered us out of the shop with no chance to say anything else. A confused Zelda and I wandered over to the van and started the engine. As I pulled onto the main street and started driving in the direction of Wildwood I looked over at Zelda.

"Be honest, what do you think the odds are of my shop still being there when we get back?"

Zelda sucked air through her teeth. "Ooh boy, I'll be straight with you Zora... I think it could go either way with that one. She can sure bake though!"

"She can," I admitted. "I have no concerns with regard to that."

"Let's just hope she doesn't get any rude customers," Zelda said. "She might torch the whole shop if pushed the wrong way."

"Yeah... that's kind of what I was worried about," I said as we drove west out of Compass Cove town.

* * *

EVEN THOUGH WILDWOOD was only about a fifteen-minute drive from Compass Cove it was wildly different in appearance and feel. Compass Cove was a built-up town next to the lake, but Wildwood was markedly more rural feeling. There were lots of farms and big open fields, and the 'center' of town was only really a couple of streets with a smattering of shops.

We drove right by all this, however. Zelda directed me to Nana Bucktooth's house, which was on the south-western edge of Wildwood town.

We turned onto a little muddy track that ran deep into some woodland, and after another five minutes of bumpy driving we finally arrived at a dilapidated wood-panel house in the middle of nowhere. The house was large, painted with fading black paint and it had a wraparound porch covered in dead leaves. Dark trees surrounded the house on all sides.

"Come on then, let's 'git inside and see what she wants already,"

Zelda said. Wildwood and its inhabitants definitely made you feel like you'd taken a step into the deep south. Just about everyone around here had a country drawl, and when Zelda came to visit hers crept out too. I found it *highly* amusing.

"Yes siree, Zelly," I said in my own mock country accent and mimed tipping a cowboy hat in her direction. Zelda just rolled her eyes and I followed up her up to the porch. She opened the front door without knocking and we went inside.

The old house's interior was just as rundown as the outside. Junk littered almost every surface, and a fine layer of dust covered everything else. The house was quite remarkable in its size, and I imagined it would look quite grand with a clean out and some fresh paint.

"Well, look what the cat dragged in," a gravelly voice said from somewhere within the room. Zelda zoned in on the voice straightaway, a scruffy cat with matted fur curled up in a fruit bowl full of mail on a small phone table. It yawned and sat up, one of its eyes was all black, the other was white with a line through it. Most of the cat's teeth were missing, the creature looked like it just got back from a ten-year vacation in hell.

"Hey Scrag, how are you doing little buddy?" Zelda said and gave the cat a scritch behind the ears.

"Oh, you know, *still* alive." The ugly cat blinked and turned its eyes on me. "Zelda please don't tell me you've cloned yourself. It didn't work, she's hideous."

"Pot kettle black," I mumbled to the cat.

"Scrag this is my half-sister, Zora. Zora this is Scrag, Maw Maw's familiar," Zelda explained.

"You look like you licked a car battery," I said to the scraggly cat. If I didn't know any better, I'd say it was only hours away from death's door.

The cat looked grossly offended by the comment. Instead of responding to me it looked back at Zelda. "Charming little thing, isn't she? Who taught her manners? A wild ape?"

"Be nice, she's new here," Zelda said. "Where's Maw Maw? She called."

"She's out back in the greenhouse. The foot massager is out there now."

Zelda took a steely breath. "Ugh, just great. Come on Zora, follow me."

Together we walked through the house. On my way out of the hallway I glared at the cat, not taking my eyes off it until we were out of the room. "There's something wrong with that cat," I said to Zelda.

"Who, Scrag? He's harmless." Zelda laughed. "He might look a little weird, but he's been like that as long as I can remember. He's a big softy really, you really have to pry it out of him though."

We passed through a kitchen that looked like it had last been decorated in the fifties and out a back door into a garden overgrown with grass and weeds. A burnt path split the overgrown lawn in two, leading to a large greenhouse at the bottom of the garden. I followed Zelda down the path and noticed how foggy it was inside the greenhouse.

"What is she doing in there?" I asked.

"She's got this wild idea that humidity is this super age reversing secret," Zelda said. "…It's kind of her thing."

"In my dream last night, she said she was on the Titanic. That was a lie, right? She'd have to be over one hundred years old."

Zelda looked back at me with her eyes wide. "She's like 120, dude. She wasn't kidding."

Well blow me down. "Is that a witch thing?"

"Nope, witches have the same life expectancy as humans. No one knows how she's doing it. My personal theory is that Death is too scared to come and get her." Zelda opened the door to the greenhouse and a wall of humid fog hit us.

"Maybe she's onto something with the humidity thing?" I asked.

"Close the door!" a voice shouted from inside. "You're letting it all out!"

We both hurried inside, and Zelda shut the door behind us. The mist obscured about ninety percent of the interior, though I could make out the silhouettes of tall plants all around us. Now we were inside I could hear Black Sabbath being blasted from a speaker.

"Hurry up then, I'm in the back!" Nana Bucktooth shouted. Zelda took my hand and led me through the misty greenhouse, as we reached the back I could just make out the old woman. She was wearing shades, sitting in an old plastic lawn chair and she was soaking her feet in a foot bath. A long brown cigarette was in her mouth, and behind her I saw two large machines blowing out sweeping curtains of humid vapor. "You've got three minutes. What do you want?"

"You brought us here," I pointed out.

Nana Bucktooth lowered her shades and looked over them at me. "I did?"

"Yeah, you did. Invading dreams, ring a bell?"

The old woman laughed and took a drag of her cigarette, the cherry burning brightly in the fog. "Oh yeah, I forgot about that."

I gave Zelda a look that said, *Is this woman for real?!*

"You mentioned something about Moon Juice going missing, Maw Maw?" Zelda prompted.

"That I did, that I did, Zelly," Bucktooth said, emphasizing each word with a point of her finger. Again she looked at me, one brow raised this time. "Does this idiot know what Moon Juice is yet?"

"Do I need to know to help you find it?" I asked dryly.

"What do you think?!" she snapped. "Of course you do!" Nana Bucktooth put her cigarette in an ashtray and sat up a little. "Zelda go and get a cannister from the back, there's one in that corner over there."

Zelda disappeared in the mist and came back a moment later holding what looked to be a large metal gas cannister. The container was painted all black with a white moon on one side and on the other in looping silver script were the words: '*Brewer Family Limited – Real Genuine Moon Juice. Since 1896*'.

"Listen up dummy, because I'm only going to explain this once," Nana Bucktooth said. "This here is Moon Juice. Invented and manufactured by the Brewer Family. Witches across the world use Moon Juice to stabilize cauldron mixtures, and to catalyze spell reactions too. Without Moon Juice a spell would take you a whole month. A little splash of our finest mixture and you can get that spell done in a matter of hours."

"Sounds impressive," I remarked. Though I knew nothing about cauldron mixing I could only imagine an ingredient like that would be mighty handy.

"It doesn't sound impressive; it *is* impressive you nitwit!" Nana Bucktooth shouted. "In the last century, the Brewer family alone is responsible for advancing magic more than any other! Several hundred years of magic achieved in a much shorter time period all thanks to Moon Juice!"

"The Brewer family must have some money if Moon Juice is so important," I commented.

"Typical Wick! Straight to the money!" Nana Bucktooth laughed in disbelief. "I'll have you know my finances are none of your business, but yes, we do very well thank you!"

I cast my mind back to the crumbling house behind me and wondered where all this money was going. I didn't put the thought into words as I suspected it would only rile the old woman up more.

"Maw Maw," Zelda said as way of breaking her out of the verbal tirade. "What's going on with the Moon Juice then?"

"Three trucks stolen in the last three months! One truck a month!" she said, holding up three boney fingers. "Now what do you think someone's doing with that much stolen Moon Juice?" Nana Bucktooth put the question to me.

"Uh… making a lot of potions?" I guessed.

She laughed. "Making a lot of potions she says. Or… they're planning to blow something up!"

"What?" I asked.

"Moon Juice is extremely volatile," Zelda explained calmly. "It's… *incredibly* explosive."

"Right…" I said, looking at the cannister of 'incredibly explosive' liquid that had been left next to a crazy old woman's still-burning cigarette. "So, someone is planning a terrorist attack." As soon as I said the words a thought occurred to me. "Wait a second, do you think this has something to do with dark witches?"

I looked at Zelda, her face rife with concern as I brought up the idea. Nana Bucktooth's face was an unreadable ocean of angry wrinkles. She nodded slowly though. "It's an idea I've entertained myself. Now if I've were you, I'd start at the Randy Wendigo. Every lowlife and criminal in this town drinks themselves to a stupor in that scum pit. I should know, I've had some great nights in there myself."

"Maw Maw, what I don't understand is why you want us to look into this? Surely Billy, Sweet John or any of the boys could dig up a thief for you?" Zelda asked.

Nana Bucktooth lowered her shades and looked at Zelda with her blown pupils. "That's just the thing Zelly. I think the thief is someone in the family."

CHAPTER 10

Back in the van, we started driving in the direction of Wildwood town.

"Just run this past me," I said, my words jittering slightly as we drove down the bumpy road. "What is the Randy Wendigo, and why are we going there?"

"It's a dive bar in town, actually it's the only bar in town. Just about everyone and their momma's been for a drink in the Randy Wendigo at some point," Zelda explained.

"Right... and why is it called that?" I asked.

Zelda shrugged. "I don't know. That's what it's always been called. Maw Maw might seem crazy, but she's right—it really is our best bet for getting answers."

It wasn't until we were back on the main road and driving into town, I realized that Zelda had produced a pair of sunglasses from somewhere, along with a baseball cap. "What are you doing? You look like a celebrity when they disguise themselves poorly."

"There's just a few folks in town that I'd like to try and avoid," she said cryptically. "So I'd appreciate if you didn't really draw attention to the getup."

"I don't think you realize how much more attention you're

drawing to yourself by wearing that 'getup'. Just take it off and you'll blend in just fine." I looked over at my sister, laughing to myself at how stupid she looked.

"Nuh uh, it stays on," Zelda said stubbornly.

"At least tell me who you're hiding from then," I reasoned.

"No, I can't tell you."

"You either tell me or the second we pull up I'm going to shout your name as we walk down the street. You know I'll do it!"

Zelda let out a sigh and I knew that she had given up. "Fine, but you don't tell Sabrina or Celeste about it. Promise me."

"Cross my heart and bake a pie," I said and crossed my chest. "Now who are you hiding from? It's a guy, isn't it?"

"I'm hiding from several people, but the main one is Sheriff Dilby. Part of the reason I moved out of Wildwood is because of him. Last time I was here things didn't end on good terms, and he said if he saw me back in town again there'd be trouble."

I laughed in response, mostly because I couldn't believe it. The Zelda I knew was a goody-two-shoes, she didn't get in trouble at all, never mind getting run out of town by the law enforcement. "These country bumpkins really bring out the worst in you, eh? What did you do exactly?"

"I didn't really do anything. Nana Bucktooth and everyone else in the Brewer family are as crooked as a fishhook, but I always kept to the straight and narrow. That's why Dilby liked me. In fact, he *really* liked me. He even went so far as getting an engagement ring and asking for my hand in marriage."

"Oh... wow," I said, driving in silence for a few seconds as I took that in. "How old is this guy?"

"Same age as me. Anyway, I said no because—well let's just say I said no because I wasn't interested in him that way. We were good friends, and that is all."

"He told you to get out of town because you declined his proposal?" I asked in disbelief.

"Uh... not exactly. Listen let's just drop it, okay? We're nearly at the bar. It's just at the end of this street so pull over and we can just get this over with."

"You're hiding something from me," I said as I examined her. I pulled up and turned the engine off.

"Can we just get out the van?" Zelda said and hurried out.

She was definitely up to something.

Zelda walked quickly down the block, and I hurried after her. I *was* tempted to shout 'Hey everyone, look, it's Zelda!' but I knew Zelda would just end up giving me grief about it.

From the outside the 'Randy Wendigo' looked like a grim little dive bar, and as we went inside that impression only doubled in my mind.

A set of steps led down to a large dark room with sticky floors and one long bar on the left wall. Ceiling fans churned slowly through cigarette smoke, country music was floating from a jukebox somewhere, and a smattering of daytime patrons were drinking quietly at their individual tables.

We approached the bar, where a bald skinny man with large spectacles was polishing glasses. "Well I'll be a skunk's uncle, it's Zelda Brewer!" he said with a huge goofball smile.

"Seriously?!" Zelda said in exasperation. She took the shades and cap off and glowered at the barkeep. "Listen up Milton we haven't got time to get cozy and talk. I'm here on family business."

Milton looked a little scared by that prospect. "Nana Bucktooth send you here?"

"You bet your sweet bippy she did! Now listen up because I've got ques—"

"Who's this?" the bartender asked, looking at me.

"Zora Wick," I answered. "I'm her half-sister."

"Half-sister! Zelda you never told me you had a—"

Zelda slammed her fist on the bar, cutting Milton's talk short. I watched quietly in amazement because I'd never seen her act like this. "Listen Milton I've got a lot to do and not a whole lot of time in which to do it. Now start talking. Someone's stealing Moon Juice, tell me what you know."

"Me?!" he laughed nervously. "What makes you think I know anything?! I just pour drinks and—"

Zelda lurched forward, grabbed Milton's shirt and pulled him in close. "Listen up Milton! It takes a big idiot to steal from Nana Bucktooth, and every big idiot in this town comes in here, gets drunk, and blabs about their big idiot schemes to all the other big idiots! You're the biggest idiot of them all, and I know you pick up every last bit of gossip with those satellite dishes you call ears, so start blabbering!"

Milton gulped down his nerves and looked at me. "Tell her to back down, she's crazy!"

I held up my hands. "Hey man I'm just here for the ride. I'd start answering questions though, I don't think she's messing around."

"I don't know who stole the stupid Moon Juice," Milton stammered to Zelda.

"But you *do* know something, so tell me what you know!" she demanded. "Or I'll get Nana Bucktooth down here herself and you can talk to her!"

Grave fear came over the bald-headed bartender. "No!" Milton said. "No, let's take it easy here! No need for that! I—I *might* have overheard a *small* thing the other night. Someone mentioned Sheriff Dilby found a stash of Moon Juice hidden in the old salt sheds by the highway."

Zelda yanked him in closer. "And?!"

"He went back to the station to get a trailer so he could confiscate the cannisters, but when he got back to the sheds the stash was gone. Someone had moved it!"

Zelda stared at Milton for a long hard moment before releasing him from her grasp and sitting back on a bar stool. Milton brushed himself off and put some distance between himself and Zelda.

I just looked at my sister in amazement. "Straight and narrow huh?" I asked her.

"You can stay quiet," she grumbled.

I didn't. "I don't know who this hardball detective is, but I am loving it," I said, pointing up and down at Zelda.

"It's this town, it brings out the Brewer in me..." she muttered as though embarrassed by the outburst. Without another word Zelda walked out of the bar and I followed her.

"So are we going to just gloss over that scene back there?" I asked as we headed for the truck. "You literally scared the truth out of that guy!"

"Milton? He's a sniveling little coward. If he's got nothing to hide, he doesn't talk at all, he's the least hospitable bartender in the country. He only starts with small talk when he knows something—that's how I knew he was lying."

"For the record I like country Zelda. She gets stuff done! You're such a shrinking violet back in Compass Cove."

"Am not!" Zelda said as we climbed into the truck. "So where to now?"

"Well it sounds like this Sheriff Dilby might have some answers..." I began.

"No, absolutely not. We are not going to see him. I'm putting my foot down on that one, and you are not tricking me into it." Zelda crossed her arms.

"Alright that's fair enough." If I was Zelda I wouldn't want to see the guy either. "The only other lead we have is checking out these old salt sheds then. Do you know where they are?"

"Yeah, I can direct you. Milton said they're empty though—can't see them being much use. What's the point of going there?"

I started up the engine and pulled onto the street. "You said it yourself back there in the bar. It takes a big idiot to steal from someone like Nana Bucktooth. I'm willing to bet that big idiot might have left something up there for us to find."

"Seems pretty thin," Zelda griped.

"That's because it's Plan B. Plan A is talking to this Sheriff Dilby." I looked over at her and smiled.

"To the salt sheds!" she said enthusiastically.

I laughed. "Yup, I thought you might change your tune."

* * *

"Are you going to tell me why you're being so secretive then?" I asked Zelda as we drove to the old salt sheds. "I mean you're obviously hiding something. What happened after you turned down this Sheriff Dilby's engagement?"

"I really don't want to talk about it," Zelda mumbled.

"Oh come on, I'm your sister!" I said to her. "If you can't talk about these things to me then who can you talk to?"

"My shrink?"

"Forget your shrink for a second. Why don't you want to talk to me about this stuff? I'm not going to blabber to Celeste and Zelda, if that's what you're worried about."

"I know you wouldn't, I just—" She paused as she put her thoughts together. "Well, I guess it wouldn't hurt to open up a little. It's weird because I don't really ever talk about this stuff with anyone."

"I'm not just anyone, dawg, I'm your sister!" I reached across and punched her in the arm playfully. "Come on!"

"Right here."

"Why not right here? No time like the present!"

"No, I mean you need to take a right here!"

I threw my hands to the right at the last second, the van careening across the road, its tires screeching under the sharp momentum. I straightened up and grinned at Zelda, who didn't look as impressed with my driving.

"So, I didn't just say no to Dilby's proposal because I didn't like him. I said no because someone else proposed to me at that time too," she explained.

"Hang on, you've had two people propose to you?" I said in amazement. "Who was the other guy?"

"Will, Will Hackerty. He was my boyfriend at the time, we were together for a couple of years. I said yes to him, we were engaged for a while but never married."

"I don't even know how to process this. You've literally had a whole other secret life. So this Dilby guy proposed to you while you were in a relationship with this Will guy?"

Zelda nodded. "Yeah. We were all friends in High School actually.

Will and Dilby used to be best friends, but that kind of ended when Will and I started dating. They're both very different people now—Dilby is the Sheriff, and Will is usually getting into some sort of trouble with my dad. Dilby proposed to me once he heard Will was going to do it. He said it was my 'last chance to do something right with my life.'"

"Yikes. I can't imagine why you didn't say yes."

"Will laughed it off when I told him about it. The two of them hate each other now, even more so after I left town"

"So, Zelda had a love triangle of her own once upon a time. How come you never married this Will? What's he like?" I asked.

"Will is... great fun, but. he has no vision for anything past today. He's a boy in a man's body. I left because I just couldn't picture spending my entire life in this town being mother to a man that I'm married too."

"Amen to that," I muttered.

"Anyway, that's the long and short of it, and now you're all caught up."

"And doesn't it feel good to unload?!" I said excitedly.

Zelda just gave me a look.

After a few minutes of silent driving Zelda pointed at a lay-by up ahead and told me to pull over. We got out of the van and through the trees on the roadside I could make out some old buildings about twenty feet from the tarmac. "Just through here, follow me," Zelda said.

It was early afternoon now; my stomach was starting to rumble, and the air was growing hot. The sky was bright blue, and a gentle breeze rustled through the trees. It was quiet and peaceful out here. We walked through the thicket and into a clearing where three old wooden sheds stood, slowly decaying through exposure to the elements. Each shed had two wooden doors that were locked together with chains and padlocks.

"No one really uses these things anymore," Zelda explained as we approached one of the locked doors. She pulled out her wand and started fiddling with the chains. "They store grit here in the winter, but the rest of the year they're empty."

"Who locks them up?" I asked.

"I imagine it's probably Polly, she's the locksmith in town."

"Is there a chance she'd know who was storing the stolen Moon Juice here?"

"I doubt it," Zelda said. The padlock opened and I helped her unravel the thick chains. "Polly's one of the few honest people in town. There's plenty of folks like me that can make short work of locks and chains with a wand. There are also plenty of non-magic folk that were taught how to pick locks as soon as they were old enough to walk."

We opened up the double doors to the sheds and stepped inside. The three units were all connected so there was no need to pick the other locks. "Looks pretty empty," I said and walked into the vacant sheds. My voice echoed slightly across the space.

There was no sign that the stolen Moon Juice had been stored here at all, just a dusty poured-concrete floor covered in dirt and traces of grit.

We both walked in and looked around aimlessly, knowing that we'd hit a dead end here. "Maybe you can go and talk to Dilby by yourself," Zelda posited. "But don't tell him anything about being related to me."

"That might be a little difficult, what with us looking identical and all." I pointed out. Zelda grimaced as she considered that truth.

"Darn, that's a good point." She let out a big sigh. "Well, I say we go and get some lunch and maybe head back to Compass Cove. We've made a little progress today, but I've got chores to do at home."

"Won't Nana Bucktooth throw a fit if she finds out we left?" I asked.

"Well, we're certainly not solving this thing today!" Zelda walked back in the direction of the doors, and I followed her.

"Yeah, it's not looking likely. Where's good to eat in town?"

"Best place bar none is Greasy Reece's, it's a diner near the lake. The food there is disgusting in the best possible way."

"Sign, me, up," I said, clapping my hands after each word. It sounded just like the thing I needed. I was just about to follow Zelda outside when something caught my eye however, a flash of blue on the ground behind one of the old wooden doors. I stopped and ducked behind the door to take a look, crouching low to the ground as I picked up the small item.

Zelda turned around and saw me holding something. "What did you find?"

"It was on the ground behind the door, right up against the wall, hidden behind one of the metal uprights." It was a small cube of bright blue pool chalk, wrapped in a vivid crimson label. Upon the label there was a picture of a red genie woman holding a pool cue, underneath her were the words 'Screaming Genie'. I relayed as much to Zelda, and she groaned upon hearing the words.

"Oh no..." she said quietly.

I looked at her upon hearing the unusual reaction. "What is it?" I asked.

"It's Will. That's his chalk."

"Your ex-fiance?"

"Yeah. He orders 'Screaming Genie' pool chalk online specially, claims that it's 'lucky'. Will never used any other chalk while playing pool down at the Randy Wendigo, and he never let anyone else touch his chalk either. He must have dropped it here by accident."

"So, this Will Hackerty has something to do with this missing Moon Juice then," I concluded.

Zelda let out a very long sigh. "Yeah, it's starting to look that way."

We both locked the shed back up and walked back to the truck to get some lunch in town. It seemed Zelda was poised for a run in with one of the men from her past—whether she liked it or not.

CHAPTER 11

After a rather amazing lunch at Greasy Reece's, Zelda and I decided to call it quits for a day with the Moon Juice mystery and we headed back to Compass Cove. Zelda assured me Nana Bucktooth wouldn't have an issue with us putting the investigation on hold for now, and she text the old woman to tell her as much.

"She has a phone?" I asked in surprise.

"Yeah, but to be honest Scrag is the one that handles it most of the time."

I knew that Zelda was mostly putting the detective work on hold because the next step involved talking to her ex-fiancé. I was tempted to give her a hard time about it, but for once I decided to let it slide.

After all I had my own problems to worry about. Daphne was locked up at the police station for a murder she didn't commit, my wand was a couple of spells away from blowing me to kingdom come, and there was a good chance I wouldn't even have a bakery to go home to, as I'd essentially left it in the hands of a somewhat questionable stranger.

I dropped Zelda off at her apartment on the way home and when I arrived at the bakery, I let out a sigh of relief to find it still standing.

My fears abated even further when I went inside and caught up with Rosie.

"There she is, the woman herself!" Rosie sang in her Irish lilt as I walked through the door. "How was your business with Nana Bucktooth?"

"Oh you know, mildly vague and threatening." I looked around the kitchen and the front of house in amazement, Rosie had cleaned the place from top to bottom. "Did you do all this?"

"I did. I sort of start cleaning whenever I have an idle moment, not that there's been many of them today mind you. We've had a good number of customers, and I've made an effort to get to know all the regulars. Did you know Mrs. Wallace has six poodles?"

"Who?" I asked.

"Old lady, fur coat, curly white hair."

"Oh… *her*. I just call her fur coat lady in my head." From Rosie's description however I knew who she meant at once. Fur coat lady had been a daily regular here since we opened. "I should probably make more of an effort to learn these people's names, right?"

Rosie ignored the question. "I also put in a tip jar, I noticed you didn't have one." She pointed at a jar on the counter which stuffed to the brim with notes and coins.

"Holy mackerel," I gasped, picking up the jar to turn it over. "This thing is packed!"

Rosie smiled and winked at me. "You'll be surprised what a bit of customer service can do. What do you say we split them fifty-fifty?"

"Split them? Keep them. You're the one that earned them," I said and put the jar back down.

"I won't argue with that one. To be honest I was hoping you'd say that anyway."

"How much did we take?" I asked. It was basically the end of the day now and the count in the register would pretty much be final.

"I've not added it up yet, but I can do it now?" Rosie suggested.

"Sounds good, I'll flip the sign and lock the door."

Once I came back to the register and saw the cash drawer open my eyes about jumped out of my head. I'd never seen it so full of notes and coins before. "What the heck?" I said. "This is all from today?"

"Sure is," Rosie said with a proud smile. "I hope you don't mind but I introduced a couple of multi-buy deals. Buy more, save more! I'm also pretty good at the upselling business. I used to work for a car dealership, so I know a thing or two about sales."

"Looks to me you know a couple of hundred things about sales. You might have to hang around and teach *me* a thing or two."

"Is that a job offer, then?" she grinned.

"Well, I… I guess it is. Are you interested?"

"I'd be lying if I said no, Zora, but the thing with me is that I like to keep moving. I don't like staying in the same place for too long. Don't get me wrong I love what you've done with the place, but I'm not sure I'm the type that can stand behind a register all day without going crazy."

A flash of inspiration struck then. "How about the bakery van? We've done a couple days out in the van, and it was a big hit. It's not been out for a while because I was short on staff. Would that be better for you? You'd move around town several times a day."

"I am *very* interested, but there's one small problem—my license is suspended for a year," Rosie said.

"You're kidding? What happened?"

"I'll tell you what happened, a deadbeat cop knocked up my little sister and walked out as soon as she told him the news! The court didn't take too kindly to me trying to run him over in my car." For anyone else the story was insane, but Rosie explained it very calmly, as if attempted vehicular homicide was a regular part of her week.

"…Right," I said, remembering that Rosie had more than one crazy streak in her. "Well uh… I guess that rules the van out then. You can work in the shop though if you can stomach being pent up inside."

She considered it, tilting her head from side to side. "I think I could handle that. Hey, you could always hire a driver? Do you know anyone? Have me out in the van with an assistant."

"No ideas jump to mind at the minute, but I'll definitely consider it. Taking two people on for the van is probably necessary anyway, it can get really busy in that thing."

Not long after that we finished the count for the day and sure enough it was a record-breaker. Even though Rosie was an unusual and somewhat unpredictable character she definitely knew what she was doing in a bakery. As long as I didn't cross her or her family, I had nothing to worry about.

"What do you say you come back tomorrow? I can show you how I do the morning bake, and you can even incorporate some of your bakes too if you like."

"Sounds good to me boss!"

Once Rosie had gone I headed upstairs to my apartment, looking forward to an evening of peace and quiet. I was in the mood for a nice long soak in the bath and an early night to catch up on my broken sleep from the night before.

As soon as the door was open, I saw the ghosts of my Aunt Constance and Sergeant Digby floating over the kitchen table once more. "There you are!" Constance said reproachfully. "We've been looking for you all day! We need to figure out what Digby and his tree wife need!"

I stood in the doorway for a second as I took in the unorthodox greeting. To be honest I'd almost completely forgot about the dryad problem, I had so many other things on my mind. "You know it would be polite to start by asking about my day?" I said, hanging up my coat and putting my bag down.

"Where are my manners?" Constance said. "How was your day?"

"Not bad actually, Zelda and I—"

"So, our latest theory is a calculator," Constance interrupted. *"That which makes one into two. That works, doesn't it?!"*

"How in flip is a calculator going to help a dryad with a magic ceremony?" I pointed out.

"Granted there are still details that need ironing out, but I don't see you bringing any ideas to the chopping block!"

"Ooh!" Digby said excitedly. He took his large, feathered hat off his head and waved it around. "What about a guillotine? Takes one thing and makes it into two!" He'd barely finished the thought out loud when the excitement on his face turned to dissatisfaction. "No, that's not it. Stupid Digby!"

"I think you both need to take a break or something. I promise I'll designate some time tomorrow to trying to figure out the dryad problem. Right now, I just need to put my feet up and relax with some peace and quiet. It's been another topsy turvy day."

"Come on," Constance said to Digby as she floated up from the table. "I know that tone, we better get out of here before the grumpy side comes out. I'll show you that roller disco rink I was telling you about earlier…"

With Constance and Digby gone I threw a frozen pizza in the oven, poured myself a glass of wine and ran a nice hot bubble bath. I was several episodes deep into the new series of Bridgerton when Hermes walked into the bathroom casually.

"Have a fun day playing Dukes of Hazard with Zelda?" he asked.

"Let's just say it was eye-opening. I learned a lot, but I can't really share any of it with you."

"If it's about the proposals I already know," Hermes said.

I almost spat out my wine. "What, how?"

"Again, the women in this family have a really big problem with sleep talking. Like, you should seriously go and see the doctor about it."

"So you knew about her engagement but never said anything?" That was quite unlike Hermes. Normally he lived for gossip.

"Nah, I guess some things just feel off limits. Obviously, she's in her head about it all. I know all about Digby and Hackerty as well, they're both a bunch of Grade A losers, not good enough for our Zelly," Hermes said staunchly.

"I had no idea you were looking out for her in that manner."

"I might be *your* familiar, Zora, but as far as I'm concerned all of you knuckleheads fall under my care. If one of you ladies goes out and marries a moron then they will inevitably become a part of my life, and I haven't got time for morons. Same goes for you too—but Blake and Hudson already have a pass in my book. Don't get me wrong, they're stupid, but in a way that amuses me. You just have to pick one now."

"I'm not picking either of them," I said. "I really wish everyone would stop trying to ship me off. Blake and Hudson are my friends, and that's the long and short of it."

Hermes stared at me for a moment. "Right… maybe set up a voice recorder then and hear what you talk about when you're sleeping at night. Doesn't sound so 'friendly' to me! I wasn't kidding when I said you gals need to see a doctor."

"Can you just leave?" I asked in exasperation. "And stop spying on me when I'm sleeping, it's creepy!"

Hermes turned and walked back through the gap in the door. "Not as creepy as the things I hear out of your mouth!"

* * *

Rosie showed up bright and early the next morning and we went through the bake together. She knew her way around the kitchen and she was a hard worker too. Any reservations I had about her unusual character were easily cast aside by everything else that she brought to the table.

"Anyway, that's why I'm not allowed within fifty meters of any Sugar-Bear Donut store in the continental united states," Rosie concluded as she reached the end of another bizarre story.

"You've had quite the life, huh?" I reflected while unlocking the front door and flipping the sign to open.

"My momma said I was cursed with the burden of an interesting soul. I never quite understood what she meant until I was older. It's like mayhem just follows me around."

"Ever since I moved here, I've been feeling that way too."

I'd just walked back to the main desk when an unexpected face walked through the front door. It was Daphne.

"Daphne!" I said, and I ran over and gave her a hug. I wasn't usually much of a hugger, but she'd had such a horrible couple of days I couldn't help feeling sorry for her. "They let you out?"

"Only on bail. As far as Sheriff Burt is concerned, I'm still suspect numero uno. I thought I might as well come back to work while this mess is all getting sorted out." Daphne noticed Rosie behind the counter and smiled unsurely. "You replaced me already?"

I looked back at Rosie and laughed. "This is Rosie. She's the newest member of the team, don't worry—you're not out of a job. We might be putting her on the baking van, though we'll need to hire a driver first."

"I can drive," Daphne pointed out.

"True, but in a perfect scenario I've got you watching the shop while Rosie handles the van."

"What about you Zora?" Rosie asked.

"As much as I'd like to dedicate myself full time to any position this town is always throwing one thing or another at me. I'll probably be chasing down ghosts, running from enchanted pigeons or some other sort of lunacy."

Both Rosie and Daphne laughed. Daphne came over to the register and shook Rosie's hand. "Looking forward to working with you Rosie."

"Likewise. If you've heard any rumors about me then disregard them. Most of them are grossly overexaggerated, apart from the story about the Ferrari in the swimming pool. The moral of that story is: don't be a douchebag 'investor' that steals money from old people."

"Rosie's has some unusual stories," I said as clarification for Daphne. "But her heart is mostly in the right place. Mostly."

Daphne chuckled. "Hey, no judgements here. According to Compass Cove Police I killed a man the other day." She stared into the distance for a second and then quietly added. "Maybe I'm not ready to joke about that one yet."

"I think we're going to make a perfect team," Rosie said to me. "She's the scary one, and I'm the brains."

"From where I'm standing from you're both pretty scary, but sure!" I replied. "I've got a bunch of nonsense to deal with today, so are you guys okay running the shop together? Rosie feel free to go over some of your sales tactics with Daphne if you like." I looked at Daphne. "We had a record sales day yesterday because of this gal."

Daphne closed her eyes and held out her hands. "Teach me thy ways master."

"Oh, it's easy," Rosie said. "Compliment the women, and flirt with the men." Rosie picked up her tip jar. "This thing will be full by noon, I promise."

"Alright I'm going to head out," I said as I headed into the kitchen. "Try not to turn my bakery into Coyote Ugly before I get back."

"Hey, those girls made good money," Daphne pointed out.

"Amen to that!" Rosie cheered.

CHAPTER 12

I grabbed my coat and bag from upstairs and decided to walk on over to Sabrina's shop. I'd promised Digby's ghost that I'd dedicate sometime today trying to figure out what his dryad soulmate needed for this magical ritual of theirs. *That which can make one into two. That which can make one into two. Just what the heck is it?!*

Just before I left Hermes came into the kitchen. "Off to earn another day of sweat on your brow?" he asked and went over to his bowl. He immediately started scoffing food.

"I'm going to try and make some progress with this dryad problem. Hermes, do we have any books in the apartment that could help me learn more about dryads?"

"Nah, probably not," he said without even looking up from his dish.

"Great. So helpful. Thanks." With that I left the apartment. Fifteen minutes later I arrived at Sabrina's shop and I found her upstairs, unloading a box of black candles onto a shelf.

She turned and looked at me in surprise. "I wasn't expecting to see you today!" she said with a smile.

"I thought I'd try and work on this dryad mystery a little. I figured something in your shop might point me to an answer."

"Ah yes...what did she need again? *That which can make one into two.* Maybe it's a pen?" Sabrina guessed.

"A pen?" I asked.

"Yeah, like... if you added a curve to the top and a line across the bottom, you could make a number one kind of look like a two..." She stared ahead for a moment before she carried on unloading candles. "I'll leave the mystery solving to you."

"For what it's worth she said she also needed copper and turquoise."

"Now *that* I can help you with. I have those things in abundance." Sabrina looked at one of the candle's she was holding. "Want one of these by any chance?"

"A candle? Sure. One can never have enough candles."

"They're not just ordinary candles, they're magical. Once you light one of these things it'll make all eggs taste like chocolate—as long as the candle is burning of course, and in the same room as you."

"...Why?" I said after staring at her for a long hard moment.

"Why do I have them? Because some genius at 'Proctor & Goldhart Enchantments' messed up while making enchanted candles. They were meant to be divination candles but came out wrong. I just picked up five hundred of these babies for a steal!"

"You think people will buy something like that?" I asked in surprise.

"Zora my entire business is built off the back of buying this type of random nonsense. People mess up all the time when making magical objects. I swoop in, buy it all for cheap and sell it on at a premium to bored witches looking for something fun to do with their evening." Sabrina threw a candle my way and I caught it. "Take one, it's on the house!"

"I'm not a massive fan of egg..." I said as I put the candle into my bag.

"All the better to take a candle. Now they'll taste like chocolate!"

"So, do you have anything that might help me work out this dryad riddle?"

Sabrina thought for a moment before nodding to herself. "You know I think I do have a book on dryads somewhere. Maybe there's something useful in there? If you give me a hand unloading the rest of these candles, I'll see if I can dig it up for you."

And so, I somehow ended up being roped into helping Sabrina unpack several boxes of the world's weirdest candles. There was a moment when she wasn't looking, so I slipped the candle she'd given me back on the shelf. I didn't exactly fancy taking one of these things home, there was no saying what other strange things it might do.

When we were done unloading the stock, I followed her back downstairs and watched as she scanned the contents of a large bookcase.

"Can I help find it? What does the book look like?"

"It's black with white lettering on the spine. It's not strictly about dryads, it's *Kosmov's Magical Compendium on Mythical Animals*. Now where is it?!" she said, running her finger back over the spines of books that she had already passed twice now.

"It's not a big deal, I can always get it from the library. I've business there anyway, Ethyl needs my help with something."

Zelda had recently taken me to Compass Cove's Magical Library for the first time, and we very quickly found ourselves 'banned for life' after accidentally sneaking into the forbidden section. Before my mother vanished, she apparently was one of the few witches in town with access to the restricted section, and Zelda and I were convinced that might give us some answers on where she went.

The head librarian was a five-year-old girl name Ethyl, who was actually an old woman cursed to age in reverse by a jaded ex-husband of hers. After Zelda and I brought her a cake and a heartfelt apology Ethyl revoked our lifetime bans and we were now allowed in the library again.

She also gave me a list of the books our mother had most recently checked out from the forbidden section before her untimely disappearance. Most of the books were about the 'Mirror Dimension', something I knew little about. All Zelda could tell me is that it was a very dangerous plane of magic that existed close to our own reality. Coupled with the fact that I saw my mother's face hiding in my mirror a few weeks ago—it seemed to suggest that maybe she was trapped there.

Ethyl had agreed to help me look into matters under her supervision, providing I helped her with a small job first. I hadn't actually been back to visit her since then, but it was on my ever-growing to-do list. I just had to stop running chores for every other person in town, and people really needed to stop killing one another around me.

"My you get around, don't you?" Sabrina remarked. "I feel like every mother and their dog has a job for you at the moment."

"Yes, it feels like that sometimes. Look don't worry about the book; I can always come back and get it another time—"

Sabrina snapped her fingers as though recalling something. "I think Celeste has it."

"Celeste?"

"Yes, I'm pretty sure I lent it to her a few months ago when she was having problems with gnomes in her garden. Typical Celeste actually, she never gives me my things back."

"Okay, brilliant! I'll go and visit Celeste then and see if I can get the book back. I'll bring it over to you once I'm done."

Sabrina clapped her hands together. "Well that's settled then! Now can I interest you in a pocket watch haunted by a 16th century milk maid? She's got some brilliant stories. They're all in Dutch, mind you." Sabrina picked up a small brass pocket watch from a cabinet next to her and held it up.

"Uh... no," I said and laughed awkwardly. "You'll have to peddle this stuff to someone else."

"Your loss. This baby will be gone by the end of the day, I guarantee it!"

As I exited Sabrina's shop to head over to Celeste's café a police car pulled up in front of me. Blake was behind the wheel, and Hudson was in the passenger seat. "Got a minute?" Blake asked.

I rolled my eyes and walked over to the car. "How did you even know I was here?"

"Zora I know where you are at all times, it's my job as your guardian," Blake said casually. Hudson leaned over to speak.

"Actually, we've just been comparing our different tracking methods. Blake here has some pretty useful magical systems in place—"

"Likewise for Hudson here." Blake yanked a thumb in his direction. "We've merged our methods a little, and now we'll both be able to track you better than ever!"

"Great," I said through gritted teeth. "That's just... fantastic. It's brilliant to see you getting on so well."

"How are things with Nana Bucktooth by the way?" Hudson asked. "Are you any closer to fixing this problem for her yet?"

Both he and Blake looked very intrigued about that question. "Yeah, any updates?" Blake added.

"What's the matter? Itching to end this curse? I thought you were getting on so well."

"We're making the best of a bad situation," Hudson said calmly. "Doesn't mean we don't want this to be over."

"Zelda and I might have a small lead. We'll probably go back tomorrow and do some more sleuthing."

"Tomorrow?!" they both said together.

"Yeah, believe it or not I have multiple things going on in my life. Now if you'll excuse me, I have to try and figure out some dumb tree riddle so I—" I started walking down the sidewalk when Blake backed the cruiser up a little.

"Actually we were hoping you could come and help us with something really quick," Blake said.

"What is it?" I asked.

"We managed to track down the sacked security guard that was caught trying to sneak into the party yesterday. He's the one that lost his wife after Patrick Black cheated with her."

"Right," I said. "I remember. So what do you need me for?"

"Come and talk to the guy with us," Hudson said. "We both know it'll go a lot smoother with you there, and the smoother this goes, the sooner your friend is in the clear."

"You're preaching to the choir, man. I wanted to work the case;

Burt threw me off it though. He said I was too close to it all and that my bias would get in the way."

"Forget Burt," Blake said dismissively. "He couldn't find his butt with his hands in his back pockets. Besides, what he doesn't know can't hurt him, and you know we'll get this thing figured out quicker if you're on board."

I tapped my foot on the sidewalk a few times as I weighed up the proposal. On the one hand I really needed to look into this dryad problem, but in my mind clearing Daphne's name and solving this murder was the bigger priority.

"Fine," I relented. "One quick conversation. But after that I'm tapping back out of this. I don't want to get on Burt's bad side—if he has one." I climbed into the back of the cruiser and Blake pulled onto the road.

"How's the case going then?" I said to them both. "Is this security guard looking like a likely suspect?"

"His name is Jack Lawson," Hudson said, turning around to talk to me. "After speaking with people at the party the other day he's one of our main leads so far. It took some time to track him down, but apparently he's set up an auto shop on the east side of town since his job with Black broke down."

"Any other suspects in the pipeline?" I asked.

"Actually yeah," Blake said. "I might have dug up something interesting. Apparently Black used to have a song writing partner, a wiry looking fella called Mitchell Murphy."

"I know him!" I said in recollection. "He used to be in Black's band but got kicked out early on." Hudson gave me a funny look. "What? I'm a fan of their music!"

"Well from what I hear there was trouble between Black and this Mitchell Murphy," Blake explained. "We didn't get a proper chance to talk with him yet, but he's on the list."

"Black's assistant, Francesca, she mentioned something about a jilted ex as well," I mentioned.

"Molly Gould?" Hudson asked. I nodded in confirmation. "Yeah, we've got her details too. Plenty to keep us busy, that's for sure."

"Did you tell her about the break yet?" Blake asked Hudson. "The photo is in the glove box." He could only make fleeting eye contact with me via the rearview mirror because he was watching the road.

"Break?" I asked.

"We had a small break," Hudson said as he opened up the glove box, pulled out a photograph and handed it to me. It was a photo of the bookcase in Black's room. "We found this photo amongst Black's possessions, here, look with this—" Hudson also handed me a small magnifying glass. "The book that was taken is there in this photo."

Sure enough with the magnifying glass I could just make out the book. It was a light brown color, with dark text on the spine. "Kleine Lügen?" I said, reading the title of the book.

"Apparently it means 'Little Lies' it's an old mystery book from Germany. Never translated into English."

"Is it valuable?" I asked. Was it possible Black had been killed because someone wanted to steal this book for its monetary value?

Hudson shook his head. "No, we did check though—I thought the same thing myself. The book isn't worth a dime however."

"Huh… that's… weird," I said, passing the photograph back to Hudson.

"Exactly what I said," Blake chipped in. "Why would someone kill Black, and then steal a random book from the room?"

"I wonder if something was hidden in the book? Maybe money or jewels."

"Funny you should mention that, we did find a carved-out book on the lower shelf. It had cash and jewels stashed inside."

"Just the one book?" I asked.

Hudson nodded. "Yeah, we checked the others. All looked normal. Why?"

"Well, it seems unlikely that Black had more than one stash book on that shelf—which makes me think the killer took this book for sentimental value more than anything else. We already know the book wasn't worth any money…" I scratched my head at the curious detail. "It does however suggest one thing."

"What's that?" Hudson asked.

"That our killer can understand and speak German."

Blake and Hudson looked at one another momentarily as the idea came to them. "I hadn't even thought of it that way!" Blake said.

I clapped my hands together. "Let's cast our minds back to the crime scene. What do we know so far?"

"The killer smoked a cigarette, they cut Patrick Black with precision, they used a steel bench scraper as the murder weapon, and they might speak German?" Hudson recapped vaguely.

"Brilliant, that's my reckoning of it all too. Did Tamara's autopsy give us any more information?"

"No," Blake said dismissively as he parked up the car. "Other than the cut on the throat she found nothing."

Looking out of the window I saw the auto shop on the other side of the street. Its large garage door was open and anyone walking past could see inside. Several cars were raised up on stands and a big man in a boiler suit and a welding mask was using an angle grinder on some body paneling. Sparks were flying everywhere.

"I'm guessing the big guy is our man," I said. Big was an understatement by the way, this guy had to be over 7ft tall and north of 350lbs. "He makes the two of you look like puppies!"

"You're riding with a werewolf and a human enhanced with super strength and speed," Blake pointed out. "I think we'll be okay. Let's go see what tiny has to say."

The three of us got out of the car and walked across the street. On our approach the huge man in the boiler suit looked our way, turned off his grinder and stood up straight. He pulled back his welding mask, revealing a pale brutish face that looked familiar with fighting. A short crop of copper red hair sat atop his large square head.

"Jack Lawson?" Blake questioned as we stepped into the shop.

"Who's asking?" he said in a deep voice.

"I'm Officer Blake, these are my associates, Hudson and Zora. We have a few questions about Patrick Black. We understand you tried to break into his mansion the other—whoah!"

Without warning the huge mountain of a man tossed the heavy

angle grinder at Blake and Hudson, who caught it and stumbled back under its weight. I jumped back to dodge them both and when I looked up again, I saw Lawson disappearing out of sight.

"We've got a runner!" Hudson shouted in excitement.

CHAPTER 13

"We better start running then!" Blake grunted as he threw the heavy angle grinder to the floor. Both he and Hudson jumped to their feet and chased after Lawson. I ran after them too, though what I thought I could contribute in this situation I wasn't really sure. My wand was still on the fritz so I couldn't reliably use magic, and Blake and Hudson were much faster than I was.

They both disappeared through the back door of the auto shop in a flash, two streaks of color blurring in front of my eyes. As I came through the door, they had both caught up to Lawson, who was sprinting down the side alley of the shop, heading for the street.

Hudson zipped in front of him to try and end the chase without a fight, but Lawson just shoulder checked him out of the way, knocking him back. I was shocked to see a regular human knock Hudson off balance so easily, and by the looks of it Hudson was surprised too.

Blake, who was still giving chase, suddenly snapped back and hit the ground, looking like he'd hit an invisible wall. I realized what had happened: Blake had reached the limits of the ten-foot curse binding him to Hudson.

"Curse that old hag!" he wailed. "Zora, do something!"

There was about twenty feet between me and the fleeing suspect. I pulled my wand out and pointed it at Lawson, shouting a curse to bind his feet with invisible rope. My rickety wand exploded, and a wobbly white missile of light whistled loudly through the air and smacked the fleeing suspect in the back. He hit the ground and went very still.

Uh...

"I said do something, Zora, not kill the man!" Blake groaned as he and Hudson both stood up.

"He's not dead! ...Probably." We all approached the large man who was lying face down on the ground. His eyes were closed and he groaned quietly before vomiting up some strange pink goop.

"Gross," Hudson said, turning his head away. "What did you do to him?"

"I was trying to bind his feet. It's this wand, it's a liability." I tucked the wand away. "What happened with the two of you? I recall you saying something about this guy being no match for you?"

"He's big, I'll give him that," Hudson said. "But he shouldn't have been able to knock us around like that. He's unusually strong."

"Let's get him back inside the shop and cuff him before he wakes up." Blake took one arm and Hudson grabbed another. "Can you do some of that mind blanking business on him?"

"Yeah, I'll undo the last five minutes, he won't remember a thing."

Together the three of us headed back inside. I held open the door and the boys shifted Lawson onto a metal chair, cuffed his hands behind his back and restrained him with some rubber hosing. Hudson noticed a chain bracelet on the man's wrist and unclasped it.

"I think I've found out where his strength came from," he said and handed the bracelet to me. It was silver and my fingertips vibrated with the presence of magic. One link had a small blue stone set into it.

"This is just like the other cursed jewelry we've come across in the town," I said. There had been a few instances now where we'd found humans with cursed magical items—items they shouldn't have access to. Just a few weeks ago I found a cursed ring on the finger of a murder victim, and there was also a necklace polluting the mind of a merfolk queen.

"I told you about my theory, didn't I?" I said to Hudson. "I think the Sisters of the Shade are deliberately flooding the town with cursed items to create unrest." The Sisters of the Shade were a group of dark witches that had showed up near Compass Cove recently. What they wanted wasn't completely clear, but they'd already attempted to recruit me and failed. It seemed they weren't the kind of folks to take no for an answer.

"Well, it's certainly working," Hudson said. "This guy sure took me by surprise. Keep hold of the bracelet for now and get Hermes to take a look at it—I want to know what it does."

"Will do," I said, slipping the bracelet into my bag. "Heads up, looks like our mechanic is waking up."

"Better erase those last five minutes…" Hudson murmured. He snapped his fingers in front of the unconscious guy's face and a shower of blue sparks fizzled through the air.

Jack Lawson opened his eyes groggily, rolling his head on his muscle-bound neck. It took him a moment to realize where he was. His body flinched, looking like he was about to run again, but the restraints held him in place.

"What happened?!" he shouted. "What's going on here?!"

Blake stepped in front of him. "My name is Officer Blake Voss. We came here to question you about your presence at Patrick Black's house the other day. As soon as I made that clear you threw an angle grinder at us, turned to run and knocked yourself out on the fender of that car over there. Now… care to tell us why you ran?"

"Untie me!" Lawson shouted again. "This is against the law; you can't do this!"

"Actually, I'm well within my rights to restrain a suspect that tries to run from the police—especially if that suspect attacks law enforcement individuals before they run," Blake explained casually. He took a step closer and crouched down. "Now tell me why you killed Patrick Black, you big ape."

Lawson lunged to try and break his restraints then, but they held tight. His pale face turned red as he strained against them. "Call me an ape again, I dare you!"

Blake stood back and laughed. "Relax! I didn't expect to get under your skin so quickly."

"Calm down," I said to Lawson. "Just tell us what you know, and this can be over and done with. Why did you kill him?"

Jack took a few deep breaths and his face returned to a more normal color. "Sorry, I just don't like being called names. My whole life I grew up taking crap from people because I was bigger. It's still a trigger for me."

"Is that what happened with Patrick Black?" Blake pressed. "He called you a name and snapped?"

The mechanic rolled his eyes dramatically. "For the love of... I didn't kill the guy; lord knows I wanted to though. He ended my god damn marriage, took my wife, took everything from me!"

"Let's just run a little recap here to show you how bad this looks," Hudson said. "Patrick Black slept with your wife. You found out and tried to kill him. You were fired, several months pass and the other day you were caught trying to break into his party. He winds up dead, we come to pay you a visit and you attack us before attempting to flee."

"First of all, when I attacked him all those months back, I wasn't going to kill the guy, just punch him until he got the message. I *did* get a couple of good hits in by the way. If the boys hadn't pulled me off him, I might have roughed him up a little more—but I wasn't going to kill him, I swear. I might look tough, but I've got no interest in going to prison. I've got a cousin on the inside, the stories that guy tells me... yeesh."

"Why run then?" I asked. "You're obviously hiding something."

The huge mechanic let out a sigh and dropped his head. "The truth is that I *did* break into the party the other day, but it wasn't to kill Patrick Black. I broke in there to steal something from him—sort of a payback for everything he did to me. I thought that was why you were here, to arrest me for that."

"Steal something?" Blake asked. "What were you trying to steal?"

"What *did* I steal, would be the better question." The mechanic jerked his head to a set of metal drawers behind him. "Third drawer from the top, small bundle wrapped in a cloth at the back."

Hudson walked over to the drawer and found the item. He unwrapped it and inside there was a little stone egg broken in two halves. On one half there was the unmistakable fossil of some sort of small reptile, surprisingly intact. "...What is this?" Hudson asked.

"They call it the 'Raptor King', it's a fossilized dinosaur egg—apparently one of the best preserved ever found. That little rock right there is worth over two million dollars."

"Holy moly..." Hudson said, suddenly looking a little more nervous to be holding such a valuable item.

"I was one of the only people to know Black even had it. Usually, he keeps it out on display, but whenever he hosted social events at his mansion, he had me put it in a safe in his garage. I knew it would be there on the day of the party, and I knew that dumb moron wouldn't have changed the code on the safe—he didn't know how, I was the one that set it in the first place. So, I broke into the garage and stole the thing—the other boys found me just as I was leaving. It was nearly a perfect crime. The egg is so small they didn't realize I had it on me, they just assumed I was there to cause trouble with Black."

"That explains why you ran from us, but it still doesn't put you in the clear," I said. "You knew how to break into Black's house undetected, and you snuck around without being caught. It's reasonable you killed Black before the others found you."

"They threw me out before that jackass got himself murdered," Jack pointed out. "Like I said I really wasn't interested in killing the guy. Not worth losing my life over. I figured I'd just rip him off instead. I'm only confessing to the theft so I'm off the hook for the murder, I understand it doesn't look good."

"You'll do time for the theft," Blake pointed out. "You're not getting out of this one so easily."

The huge mechanic shrugged. "Eh, I'm past the point of caring. Knowing that slimeball is dead made my year anyway, he deserved everything that came to him. Listen, can we just hurry up and get this over with? I'm dying for a cigarette."

"Nicotine can wait," Hudson said sternly. "There's every chance you might be the killer."

Looking over Jack's shoulder I noticed a trashcan overflowing with takeout food containers. "You're a junk food fan I see."

He turned to see the trashcan and looked back at me. "Uh, I guess. More so that I can't cook to save my life. I could burn water. I either eat out at restaurants or go to the drive thru. Is judging people's eating habits part of an interrogation now?"

I clasped my hands behind my back and walked around the garage as I put my thoughts together. "The question is relevant actually." I stopped and looked at the under carriage of a bright blue sportscar that was currently lifted into the air. "How long have you been working on cars?"

"All my life really. My father was a mechanic, and I picked it up from watching him."

"My dad was a dab hand with cars actually," I commented. "He taught me a thing a two." I pivoted on my heels to look back at Jack Lawson. "He said a good mechanic has a steadier hand than a brain surgeon."

Lawson laughed as though in agreement. "Well, your old man had his head screwed on straight. Taking an engine apart and putting it together again isn't as easy as people think." He looked over at Blake and Hudson, seemingly confounded by my line of questioning. "Are we done here or what? What's with all these random questions?"

"Oh, she has a method," Blake said. "Sometimes we even understand it."

"Most of the time we don't though," Hudson added.

"One last thing Mr. Lawson." Walking back over to his chair I pulled out my phone and typed something on the screen. "If you can read this to me, we'll drop the charges for the stolen fossil and release you with no further questions."

"Zora!" Blake said with alarm. "We cannot do that!"

"Relax, I know what I'm doing." I turned my phone around so the mechanic could see the words I had typed out. He leaned in close and squinted and read the words poorly.

"Du bist ein Affe?" he said, long protracted pauses between each mispronounced word.

"Yes, translate that for me and we'll drop the charge and let you go."

Lawson sat back again; his brow creased with confusion. "Listen lady I have no idea what is going on here." He looked at Hudson and Blake again. "Just take me to the station already, I've had it with this crazy broad."

Blake looked at me. "Are we done here, Zora?"

I nodded. "Yeah we're done, you can arrest him… on a charge for theft."

And so, Blake cuffed the mechanic and led him to the back of the cruiser with Hudson's assistance. Before they closed the door, I stopped them. "Wait, wait."

"Lord give me strength," Lawson said. "Just take me away already!"

"One last thing, where did you get that wrist bracelet?"

"A customer gave it to me a few weeks ago as payment. I've felt… strong since I put it on."

"What did she look like?" I asked.

He thought about it but shook his head. "I can't remember actually. It's weird. I just remember she had a cloak with a hood."

Hudson, Blake, and I all exchanged a knowing glance. "Alright then." With that Blake closed the door and we drove Jack Lawson to the station. Once he was inside a cell I stopped outside to talk with Blake and Hudson.

"Care explaining what that was all about? The phone trick I mean," Blake asked me. I could see from the look on his and Hudson's face that they were both thoroughly lost.

"Just doing simple detective work boys. I think he *was* there to rob the egg, though I think it was unlikely he was the killer."

"How in the heck did you come to that conclusion?" Hudson asked.

"Yeah, please enlighten us," Blake mirrored.

"Tamara already told us the killer had a steady hand, evidenced by the precision cut to the carotid artery. Now Mr. Jack Lawson here obviously had a steady hand, evidenced by his ability to take cars apart and put them back together again. He was also a smoker, and if you recall there *was* a cigarette found at the crime scene."

"So, it was him," Blake said. "All the evidence points to him!"

Hudson nodded his head in agreement. "It sounds like you're arguing *for* the guy here, Zora, not against him."

"Well, I'm not finished. There are two points against him, however. The trashcan full of junk food alone is a big one and—"

"Wait a second," Hudson said, holding his hand up. "In what universe does a trashcan full of junk food rule someone out for murder?"

Blake thumbed at Hudson. "What he said."

"Can't you see it? A guy that lives on takeout food isn't going to have ready access to a bench scraper, which was the murder weapon, need I remind you. The person that killed Patrick Black had that item on them for a reason, and our suspect is someone that knows their way around a kitchen. Jack Lawson did not, therefore I find it highly unlikely he would have such a tool on his person."

"A person like Daphne might?" Blake suggested. I shot him a disapproving look and he held his hands up. "I'm just joking! What was with that final display of yours? Telling him we'd drop the charges if he could read those words on your phone."

I looked at both of them, feeling slightly amused. "Really, neither of you understood? I thought with your Germanic heritage you might, but he *did* butcher the pronunciation." I pulled out my phone and showed them the words.

"Du bist ein Affe?" Blake read slowly, butchering the sentence just as poorly as Lawson had. "German, right?" he asked.

"Yes! Neither of you knows what it says?"

They both looked at one another and shrugged. "Zora, we have German heritage," Hudson said, "it doesn't mean we know a thing about the language."

"Well, it appears our mechanic friend doesn't either. After all I made a bargain with him, translate the words and you're free to go. He doesn't know German, and we know that our killer likely did because they took a German book from Black's shelf."

"I think there's a flaw in your logic, Zora," Hudson pointed out. "If Lawson translated your sentence, he's basically confessing to killing Black. It makes it very likely that he's the person to take the book."

"Yeah," Blake agreed. "He could just pretend he didn't understand what you typed out and take the lesser punishment."

"You are both entirely correct, but you fail to account for one thing, our mechanic friend had rather thin skin. If he could really understand the language, I think his anger would have gotten the better of him."

Hudson's brow creased in confusion. "What exactly did you write?"

"Du bist ein Affe," I recapped. "You are an ape."

Both Blake and Hudson shook their heads in disbelief. "You saw the way he reacted when I called him that," Blake said. "Do you have a death wish?"

"Nah, I just took a gamble and it paid off. Besides, I needed it to be something that would provoke a reaction, so I could tell that he was telling the truth. Lawson might line up with a few of the clues, but I don't think he's the man we're looking for."

"Then we need to keep looking," Hudson said, turning to look at Blake. "Who's next on our list?"

"Jilted lover... spurned business partner... take your pick. Zora, what do you think?"

"I think I'll leave it with you gentlemen," I said as I started in the direction of the sidewalk.

"What? You're going?! I thought you were helping!" Blake said in disbelief.

"Yeah dude, but I've got things to do, like solving a dryad riddle."

"That's it?" Hudson balked.

"That's the tip of the iceberg, buddy. Don't even get me started on

Bucktooth, or the fact that I need to do some serious studying for magic school. I need to prepare so I don't accidentally flush the entire town down a blackhole next time I have a lesson."

Though life would certainly be easier if that happened.

CHAPTER 14

"What's the book called again?" Celeste asked as she darted around behind the counter in her café. Her shop was heaving, and a steady line of customers were waiting at the register. I was standing off to one side, distracting her as she worked.

"It's uh…" I pulled out the crumbled up note in my pocket and tried to decipher Sabrina's chicken scratch writing. *"Kaleb's Mongoose Chapel on Mystical Angles."*

Celeste did a double take and smirked. "What? Let me have a look at that." I placed the note down on the countertop and she glanced at it briefly.

"Ah, *Kosmov's Magical Compendium on Mythical Animals,*" she said with a tone of familiarity. "Man, Sabrina's handwriting is terrible. I think I'm the only one that can read it apart from mom."

"Do you have the book then? She said you were the last one to borrow it. I need to try and figure out what these dryads want if I'm ever going to get my wand fixed."

Celeste loaded up a tray with two plates of pie and called for the next customer. Once she'd taken the order her attention was back on me. "I'll be honest I don't remember borrowing that book. I borrow a lot of things from Sabrina, I kind of lose track of things."

"Yeah, Sabrina said you never give things back," I said without thinking.

"She said what?!" she said, her eyes growing wide. "That's rich coming from the woman that still has my Bridget Jones boxset!"

"Hey, don't shoot the messenger!" I held up my hands as if in surrender. "You don't remember borrowing the book then?"

"Nah, but if you see Sabrina before me then tell her I want that boxset back," Celeste said, pirouetting between countertops while getting orders ready at lightning speed.

I smiled awkwardly at the customers waiting and lowered my voice a little. "She said uh…" I dropped my voice to a whisper now, hoping that the ambiance and clatter of the café would cover up my words. "She said you borrowed the book when you had a problem with garden gnomes."

Celeste stopped in her tracks for a moment before carrying on with her work. From the look on her face, I knew that I'd jogged her memory. "Actually, now you mention it I *do* remember borrowing that book from her."

"Great! So where is it?"

"I uh… don't have it," she said with a sheepish grin.

"You're kidding?!"

"No, but have no fear, I remember who *does* have it. None other than your boneheaded sister, Zelda!"

"Zelda, why does she have it?" I asked.

"I can't remember, I think it was something to do with a ghoul in her fridge? She's always got something crazy going on at that creepy little apartment of hers. She really needs to move. It's her day off, so she's probably there now."

"Alright, thanks Celeste. I will swing by now and see if Zelda can be of any help."

A few minutes later I arrived at Zelda's apartment, pressed the button and waited for the buzzer.

"Hello?" her voice came over the tinny speaker.

"Yo, it's Zora. Buzz me in, I need to grab a book off you."

"Okay, but you're not allowed to laugh."

Laugh?

The door clicked open, and I made my way upstairs, all the way to the top floor. Zelda's apartment was bizarre, for lack of a better word. It was so narrow you could stick your arms out and touch both walls, but long enough that it could fit a kitchen, a living room, a bedroom and a bathroom. It felt like two freight containers joined together at each end.

The apartment had apparently once been owned by Compass Cove's Station Master, and at his instance iron rods ran up the length of the building, from the subway station down below. This meant that every time a train went by underground anyone in Zelda's apartment heard and felt it.

She really needed to move.

I reached Zelda's apartment door and she opened it tentatively by a crack. "Promise you're not going to laugh."

"I promise I'm not going to laugh," I repeated in a droll manner. "Now can you open up already?"

The door opened and there stood Zelda in a short dressing gown. Her legs and upper lip were covered in hair removal wax, and I thought this was the thing she was embarrassed about until I noticed her hair. "Zelda, your hair is silver!" I gasped.

She yanked me inside and shut the door behind me. "I'm well aware, don't tell the whole neighborhood!" she hissed.

"But... why?!" I said in disbelief.

Zelda let out a long sigh and I followed her to the bathroom. Her mirror was surrounded by all sorts of bottles and boxes. "When I was sixteen, I tried out this spell to change my hair color and messed it up. Ever since then my hair has been bright silver—nothing I can do changes it back, not even magic. I have to take a day off once a month to wash out the dye and reapply it all."

"For what it's worth I think the silver is a killer look on you," I said sincerely.

"I appreciate it, but I'm not ready to be a silver fox yet. Sometimes life just feels unfair." Zelda pulled two plastic gloves on her hands and started smearing dark brown dye through her hair. "Anyway, you said something about a book?"

"Ah, yes." I pulled Sabrina's crumpled note out of my pocket again before stopping myself. I was pretty sure I could remember the title by now. "I'm looking for a book to learn more about dryads. Sabrina recommended this one, *Kosmov's Magical Compendium on Mythical Animals*. She said Celeste had it, and Celeste says *you* have it."

"Yes," Zelda said while bundling her hair up with a bobble.

"Yes?" I questioned.

"Yeah, there was this ghoul in the water boiler. Kept freezing the hot water and banging the pipes. I stuck him with a shrinking spell and trapped him in a jar. He's still on my bookcase actually, I probably need to upgrade his jar to something more secure..."

"But you have the book?" I asked.

"Oh yeah, it's on the bookshelf too, I think. Give me a minute to put this on and I'll come and find it for you. Why don't you make us a cup of tea? I'll only be five minutes."

So, I made us a cup of tea while I waited for Zelda to do... whatever she was currently doing to her hair. Five minutes later she came out of the bathroom, grabbed the cup of tea I made her, and I followed her to the bookshelf.

"There he is," she said, pointing at an old jam jar on the bookshelf. Inside there was a small silver ghost floating with its arms crossed, a sour grimace fixed upon its face. "Doesn't feel so good now, does it?!" she said, taunting the small specter.

"Shouldn't you free that thing?" I asked.

"The ghoul? Nah. They're horrid things. Plus, it's good to have one around, it stops others from coming in. These buggers thrive on mischief and trouble—I guess you have a lot in common actually."

"Ha ha," I said sarcastically. "Now do you have this book or not?"

Zelda scanned the bookshelf for a minute before stepping back and folding her arms. "Huh, I could have sworn it was here."

I couldn't help groaning. "I'm never going to find this book, am I?"

"If it's not here then I must have given it back to Sabrina, though I don't remember giving it to her. Wait! I remember now. I did give it away, but it wasn't to Sabrina."

"Who did you give it to then?"

"Hermes."

"Hermes?!"

"Yeah, it was about a year or so ago, just before Constance died. I think they had a small problem with Ding Grubs, or something like that."

"Ding Grub? What in the name of Miley Cyrus is a Ding Grub?"

"They're like these small little worms that eat sound," Zelda said casually.

"They *eat* sound? How is that possible?"

Zelda waved her fingers in the air and grinned like an idiot. "With magic Zora, anything is possible!" She composed herself. "They can be quite horrible actually. You think you're going deaf but actually they're just making like this magical sound vacuum—we had them one year at magic camp."

"The more I learn about this world of magic, the less I want to live in it," I said.

Zelda laughed while drinking her tea. "Yeah... sometimes I think about how easy the mortals have it, living in their blissful ignorance. I wouldn't have silver hair either. Still, I guess magic does have some perks."

I picked up my bag with a huff, preparing to leave yet again. "Well, let me know when you find out what they are."

"You're not sticking around?" Zelda asked.

"Nah, I've got things to do. I guess I should go back to my own house for this book. I wish Hermes had told me about it in the first place, save me trapezing all around town."

"When has Hermes ever made anything easy?" she pointed out.

"Good point," I said and opened the door. "Listen, I know you're keen to avoid it, but we should probably head back over to Wildwood tomorrow and look around for the Moon Juice a little more. I don't want your Maw Maw showing up in my dreams again."

"I have the afternoon off," Zelda said with a groan. "I guess we can go then."

"Good! And maybe text her to let her know we haven't given up. That woman scares the life out of me."

"You and me both sister," Zelda said wistfully.

* * *

On my way back to the apartment it started raining. By the time I made it through my front door I was dripping wet and feeling a little bit cold. I found Hermes reading the newspaper at the kitchen table.

"Back from another day of hard work, eh?!" he chuckled.

I shut the door behind me and hung up my things. "Do you know any good ways to skin a cat?" I asked him.

Hermes looked up from his paper and gulped. "What did I do now?"

"*Kosmov's Magical Compendium on Mythical Animals,*" I said, crossing my arms.

A clueless expression consumed Hermes' face. "Uh... a very fine book," he said. "I think we have a copy around here somewhere actually."

"We do, it's Sabrina's copy. She lent it to Celeste, who lent it to Zelda, who lent it to you when Constance was having a problem with—"

"Ding Grubs!" Hermes said heartily. "I remember now. Man, what a nightmarish couple of weeks that was. Constance and I thought we were losing our minds."

"Hm," I said, walking forward to the kitchen table. "Do you remember what I asked you when I left this morning?"

Hermes thought about it for a moment before shaking his head. "I don't remember seeing you this morning."

"Before I walked out of that door, I said, 'Hermes, do we have any books in the apartment that could help me learn more about dryads?' and you said..."

"I said 'Yes! Of course, we do, Zora!' Because I'm a very helpful familiar." Hermes grinned at me sheepishly.

"Actually, you said, 'Nah, probably not,' and then you went back to scoffing your breakfast."

"That *does* sound like something I would do," he conceded.

"So I've been skipping all over town looking for a book that was in the apartment all along, all because you neglected to mention we already had it."

He nodded for a moment. "I can see how I come out of this situation looking bad. But I might be able to make things better."

"I'm listening," I said.

"How about I fetch you the book, *and* I sing you the Chicago soundtrack from beginning to end." Hermes delivered the suggestion with a huge grin on his face.

"Get the book, forget about the singing, and maybe then I'll consider forgiving you."

He looked confused. "So, *no* singing? Alright then…I'll go and get the book."

"Oh, before you go." I pulled the cursed bracelet out of my pocket. "One of our suspects was wearing this. What is it?"

"Hm," he said as he came in close and looked at the bracelet. A smile came over his face. "Quite a handy little item actually. As far as cursed jewelry goes this is one of the better ones. It's a bracelet of strength."

"That's it?" I asked. "No other ill effects?"

He narrowed his eyes, studying some invisible element that I couldn't detect. "Maybe it lowers inhibition slightly? Apart from that, this is a pretty neat find."

"It explains how that guy body checked Hudson out the way at least. Okay, thanks. Can I have this book now?"

"What did your last servant die of?" he joked. Hermes skittered out the room and I took a seat at the kitchen table. He'd barely left when Constance and Digby raced through the kitchen wall, looking out of breath.

"For the love of—" I said, jumping slightly at their rapid entrance. "Why are you panting? Can ghosts even get out of breath?"

Both the ghosts straightened up as they considered the question, and they suddenly stopped the panting. "Guess it's an old habit," Constance reflected.

"Guess so," Digby agreed.

"What's with the white-knuckle appearance anyway?" I asked them. "Why did you both rush in here so quickly?"

Constance swathed a hand through her ghostly hair. "We were at the cemetery trying to figure out this dryad riddle."

"We thought we might ask a couple of the old ghosts around there," Digby said. "See if they know anything about it."

"Any luck?"

"Uh… not exactly," Constance said. She and Digby both looked at one another. "Let's just say we won't be going back to the cemetery for a while."

"What did you do?" I groaned.

"Nothing they didn't deserve!" Digby boasted, drawing his saber and thrusting it into the air.

"Will you be quiet!" Constance said, smacking Digby's sword out of the air. She turned and looked at me with the look of someone that was neck deep in trouble. "There's a small chance we may have disturbed the tomb of the Black Abbot by accident…"

"Who now?"

"The Black Abbot," Digby repeated and put his sword back into its sheath. "Story has it that he ran a monastery around these parts, several hundred years ago—before my time even. He and his monk brethren went mad and conducted all sorts of dark experiments in their abbey."

"What kind of dark experiments?" I gulped.

"Oh, the usual," Digby said casually. "Abducting humans, using magic to turn them into gruesome creatures. You know that sort of thing. The story goes that they were possessed by dark forces."

"Anyway," Constance interjected, "The townsfolk put a stop to it eventually, the Black Abbott and his entire monastery were hung and quartered. Their remains were sealed away in a tomb to stop them from ever coming back."

"And you just disturbed this tomb?" I said with a blank look on my face.

"Yes, but in our defense, it *was* an accident," Constance said.

"And we fixed it straightaway!" Digby added hastily.

"Besides, it's just an old tale to scare naughty kids. There's nothing to worry about!" Although Constance said the words, it didn't sound like she believed them.

"If that's the case then why did you both hotfoot it back here?" I pointed out.

"Ah well that's easy to explain—" Digby said. "The other ghosts in the cemetery chased us here. They weren't too happy about us almost releasing a group of evil spirits."

"Imagine that," I muttered.

Hermes came pattering back into the room, a large book floating in the air behind him. "And the award for familiar of the year goes to, Hermes Wick!" Hermes jumped up onto a kitchen chair and set the book down in front of me.

"Thanks, but you get a participation award at best," I said with a scowl.

"Ouch, don't hold back!" Hermes cried.

Constance scoffed at him. "You never cared about the familiar of the year award before, why start now?"

"That's an actual thing?" I asked as I flipped open the book.

"Yes, but it's rigged," Hermes spat. "Why else would little miss perfect paws win every year?"

"Who?"

"Princess Sparks," Constance explained. "She's the familiar to Honey Sparks, another Prismatic witch from Australia. They're both insufferably perfect. Honey Sparks is just about the most famous living witch today, and everyone loves her. Her familiar wins every year."

"It's rigged, rigged I tell you!" Hermes wailed.

"Quiet down already, with any luck I can figure out this dryad nonsense and be done with it." I looked up at Digby and gave him an apologetic smile. "No offense."

"None taken my dear, none taken."

Hermes, Constance and Digby all busied themselves with conversation around the table while I flicked to the entrance about dryads to see what the book had to say:

'DRYADS ARE TREE SPIRITS, *sometimes known as nymphs or human trees. They are reclusive creatures, opting to live in remote areas of nature, typically in heavily forested areas to help give them natural cover. While they are usually quite neutral, dryads* will *attack if they feel threatened or confronted. Forge a relationship with them however and the dryad can be a powerful ally. It is said a branch from their bodies can be used to make powerful wands.*

Dryads typically live in groups of 10-30 and will establish a settlement around a small body of luminescent magical water, which they help to create with their collective powers. The water, known as a 'Beatha' to the dryads, provides magical sustenance to the group, and also serves as a way for them to check their reflections. (Although dryads reportedly have a reputation of being wild in appearance, I found them to be incredibly vain creatures. They will spend many hours a day staring at their reflections in the surface of the Beatha water.)

To this date, it is not yet known how dryads come into existence, though some speculate they come to life under a full moon, when a normal tree is wrapped with copper and turquoise stones. (For more information on dryads refer to my other book: A Fortnight in the Forest: Two Weeks Witching with Tree Folk.)

- *Gwenda Kosmov.'*

AS I FINISHED READING the entry it was like the answer to Glau's riddle came to me immediately. I slammed the book shut and couldn't help letting out a little laugh. "I can't believe it. It's so obvious! *That which makes one into two!*" I stood up from the table and started in the direction of my bedroom to get a good night sleep.

"You cracked it?" Constance said. "What's the answer!"

"Digby, go back to the forest and tell your betrothed I'll be there tomorrow with the items." I chuckled again and shook my head. "I can't believe I didn't figure it out earlier."

"Zora, Zora!" Hermes shouted from the kitchen. "You can't leave us hanging like this!"

"Just watch me!" I shouted back.

CHAPTER 15

"Hello?" Blake said as he answered the phone the following morning.

"Hey, it's Zora. I need your help with something. I'm going back to Fog Death Forest. I've figured out what the dryads need."

"Wait a second, let me get this straight. You're about to go and do something dangerous and you're telling me about it beforehand? Who are you and what have you done with Zora?" he joked.

"I know right? I'm turning over a new leaf. Can you help me or not? Once I've helped the dryads I can get a new wand, and once I've got a new wand, I can help you and Hudson out and break this joining curse."

"You strike a hard bargain, though I'm going to insist we get more help on this mystery case too. Hudson and I are spinning in circles with this thing."

"Fine, I'll help out with that too. I'm going over to Sabrina's now and we'll be at the forest in about half an hour. Can you meet us there?"

"Sure can. See you soon."

After that I got in the van and headed over to Sabrina's. I told her what the mystery item was last night via text. Constance and Hermes I'd left to wallow in their misery overnight—I saw it as payback for them both making my life so difficult.

"Rise and shine!" I said cheerily to Sabrina as I walked into her shop. She was in her dressing gown and sipping a cup of coffee behind the counter.

"S'morning," she yawned. "Are those donuts for the taking?"

"Sure are," I said and plopped down a box of donuts that I'd baked this morning. "Why are you so tired?"

Sabrina took a donut and shoved it into her mouth. "It turns out those candles that make eggs taste like chocolate also scream at night. It's… been an interesting couple of hours. I'll have to box them up today and send them back. No way I can sell any more of those."

I smirked. "How many did you sell?"

"Close to twenty yesterday. I can see a lot of angry customers in the shop today asking for refunds."

I was glad I'd stealthily put my candle back on the shelf. "All the better for us to go out of town to a deadly forest, eh? Blake and Hudson will be escorting us this time—formally. Have you got the things ready?" I asked.

"It's all in a box out back. Let me finish this drink, throw on some clothes and then I'm good to go. Say, didn't your candle keep you up all night with its screaming?"

"I uh… I just assumed it was Hermes being his old self. It's practically background noise to me now."

"Clearly I need to get an annoying familiar," Sabrina yawned.

"I have the perfect candidate if you're interested."

Not long after that we packed our items into the back of the van and drove out to Fog Death Forest. As we pulled into the quiet dirt parking lot, we found Hudson and Blake were already there, looking over some files they had open on the hood of Blake's cruiser.

"Bit of light reading?" I asked as we got out of the van.

"Just going over the case again while we've got a quiet moment," Blake said. "We ready to do this?"

"Sure are," I said. "Could one of you help carry the things? It's quite bulky."

"Where's Celeste and Zelda?" Hudson asked.

"They're in the café today. Celeste said they couldn't close, they've already lost too much business this week," I explained. To be honest I didn't blame her. It really felt like I was becoming a burden on everyone.

"Less people to get mauled," Blake said with a shrug. "Let's unpack this stuff."

After the van was unloaded, we set off into the forest, heading in the direction of the dryad camp. After about fifteen minutes of walking Constance and Digby appeared, both looking quite excited about the morning's events.

"We've scanned the perimeter and there's nothing concerning nearby!" Constance said enthusiastically. "Well, there is a Spriget about two miles west of here, but it's walking in the opposite direction."

"What's a Spriget?" Sabrina asked. After seeing Hudson's confused look, she elaborated. "Constance just appeared. She says there's one nearby."

"Ah. In some cultures, the Spriget is known as the Mongolian Death Bird. Very interesting creatures actually," Hudson said casually. "They hypnotize you with their eyes, get you to smash your own head open with a rock and then they peck your brain out. Quite remarkable creatures." We all stared at him for a moment, and he shrugged. "What? I had to deal with a pack of them once. They're dangerous, but they have impressive plumage."

"That about settles it, you're definitely a psychopath," Blake said.

"Says the guy who puts milk in the bowl before cereal," Hudson replied.

Everyone in the group seemed more alarmed by this than Hudson's brain-eating bird. "What?!" came a collected outcry.

"It works out better in the end!" Blake argued. How that was true I couldn't possibly tell.

One thing I'd noticed since these two were stuck together is how well they were getting on now. Part of me didn't want to end the curse keeping them bound within ten feet of the other, because things had never been as good as they were now. On the other hand, I knew it wasn't 'normal' and they couldn't go on living like this forever, but it was mighty tempting to leave things as they were.

Before long we arrived at the dryad camp, with the turquoise, the copper, and *'that which can make one into two'.*

"Finally!" Glau celebrated as we stepped into the clearing. "You have the items we need for the ceremony! Set them down against that sapling over there!"

Blake and Hudson set down the mystery item, which we had wrapped in cloth to protect it. They stood it up against the tree and removed the cloth.

"Just a heads up," I said to Glau. "In human tongue we call this mystery item a *mirror.*"

"Yes, mirror!" Glau cheered as if recalling the name. "That which can make one into two!" She churned across the ground and stopped in front of the mirror to regard her own reflection. "Look! Now there are two of me, marvelous!"

"I can't believe I lost sleep over this," Constance groaned.

With the mirror resting against the sapling, I handed Glau the turquoise stones and the copper bands. We all stood back and watched as the dryads wrapped the strands around the sapling and placed the turquoise stones at its roots. Digby's ghost floated in front of the mirror and the dryads began a strange and ritualistic chant, their melodic words weaving through the air as a magical song.

The mirror, which was just an old thing Sabrina pulled out of the attic, began to glow bright green and Digby's ghost passed through the reflective glass. As he did the mirror dissolved in a flash of blinding green light and his ghostly form dissolved into the sapling behind it.

The tree began to grow until it was the same height as the other dryads, its branches and roots twisting rapidly until the familiar face of Digby emerged from the trunk. It was a sapling no more, but a new dryad.

"The ceremony is complete!" Glau cheered, the rest of her the tree folk in the clearing all shouting in unison. She embraced Digby in his new form, their branches furling around one another and their trunks drawing close.

Once the celebrating was done Glau came over with a branch of wood glowing with green light. "As promised, we uphold our end of the bargain. This branch comes from Merrydod, one of the oldest amongst us. May the magic in this wood bring you great power."

"Thank you," I said as I took the gift. The bark was warm to the touch and my fingers crackled as I felt the powerful magic lurking beneath the surface. "I will be much more careful with this one, I promise."

Not long after that we left the camp and made our way back through the dark forest. "Well, that was without doubt one of the weirdest things I've ever seen," Blake muttered.

"Eh, just a normal day for me," Hudson remarked. "I had no idea that's how dryads were made."

"I don't think it's commonly known," Sabrina pointed out. "It's always been a mystery."

"I remember reading that in the book actually. That guide by that Kosmov woman? She said no one knows how dryads are made," I said.

Sabrina suddenly became excited. "Ooh! We should totally write in and tell her! We could get a reader bounty!"

"A what now?"

"A reader bounty! If you write in with new information about a topic you can be rewarded with a prize!"

"Ooh. Well, I do like positive reinforcement with physical prizes."

Soon after that we made it through the forest without being accosted by horrible magical creatures and made it safely back to the lot. "So, up for a bit of sleuthing?" Blake proffered.

"I *am*, but I did promise I'd help Zelda out with this Nana Bucktooth thing first. If I get back soon enough, I could help you out later?" I suggested.

"That could work," Hudson said. "Just give us a call when you get back into town."

After we said our goodbyes, we got into our vehicles and headed back in the direction of Compass Cove. I had to take Sabrina back to her shop and then go to the café to pick up Zelda.

"So, how long do you think the wand will take?" I asked as I pulled up outside Wytch's Bazaar.

"It won't be ready overnight, that's for sure. Getting the wood was one thing, making the wand is another thing altogether," Sabrina explained.

I groaned. "Please don't tell me we have another shopping list full of riddles."

"No riddles. Don't worry about this next part, I'll source the things I need. I have some of them already. It's slightly more difficult to make a prismatic wand, I need a few materials in place to make sure my wand lathe doesn't turn this town into a small crater."

I'd seen Sabrina use her wand lathe once. Residing in her basement, it looked like a cannon that had been ripped off a battleship. Sabrina sat in a tiny cabin on top of the machine, struggling with a cockpit of confusing controls while the machine spun around and belched fire and smoke, like a mechanical bull on a bad acid trip.

"...Okay. Well, let me know if there's anything I can do to help! If I knew making these things was such trouble, I'd never have broken the last one."

"Eh, breaking that wand saved all of our lives. I think you made the right call. I'll get started on the wand today, but I'm getting rid of these screaming candles first."

"If I had a nickel every time I heard somebody say that!" I joked.

* * *

"Holy moly! Watch out Jessica Simpson!" I gawped as Zelda climbed into the van. If I hadn't just picked Zelda up from a shift at her café, I would thought she'd been on a three-day 'Little Miss Country' makeover. Her hair and makeup were done to perfection, and she was wearing skintight jeans, a plaid blouse unbuttoned over a white tank top, and a tan cowboy hat with matching boots.

"Quiet down," Zelda mumbled, pulling her cowboy hat down slightly over her face. "Celeste already made a big enough fuss; I don't want to hear the same from you!"

"You just look a little different to usual," I said as I signaled and pulled out onto the street. Zelda's everyday wardrobe was very much in the same camp as mine—dress, cardigan, and boots—I'd never seen this side of her before.

"Yeah well, what would you wear if you were going to knowingly run into your ex? Back in Wildwood this is how the women dress, and if I want to get answers out of Will then I need to dress to impress."

"Consider me impressed. You look like a total babe, and I mean that sincerely."

Zelda looked over at me and actually let out a little smile. "Thanks, I guess," she mumbled. "So, let's change the subject. What's the plan?"

"*My* plan was to go and weasel some answers out of some dumb hillbilly dude, but now we've got Miss Texas on our side I think we can let the booty do all the talking!"

Zelda glared at me and turned the radio on. "Enough of the jokes now!"

"But I've got like twenty more at least!" I sighed. "If you get to play Shania Twain today at least you could involve me."

"You've got a wand, use it!" Zelda said.

"And turn myself into a bullfrog? Nah ah. Do it for me!"

With a *'Do I have to'* eyeroll, Zelda pulled out her wand and flicked it lazily in my direction. Magic light shimmered over my body and turned me into a cowgirl too, but I didn't look anywhere near as glamorous as she did.

"Yee haw!" I crowed and pounded the horn a few times. "Let's go tie up some hogs then!"

"You are so embarrassing," Zelda grumbled and sank into her chair.

Several songs later we arrived in Wildwood town, and I'd somehow successfully bit my tongue for the entire ride and kept back the torrent of jokes that wanted to break free. Zelda had a habit of being a little sensitive sometimes, and I knew I could only make so many jokes at her expense before she started getting really cranky.

The truth was she did look really great, and I knew that facing an ex was never an easy thing. If this guy so much as said a word to make her upset, I had no reservations about using my messed-up wand on him, even if there was a chance he might get teleported all the way to China.

"So where do we find this Will Hackerty?" I asked Zelda.

"The Hackerty family farm is a good place to start. The Hackery's and the Brewers are closely intertwined—one day they're enemies, the next day they're best friends. Will actually works at the Moon Juice plant with my dad, Billy Brewer. Billy's got twenty years on Will, but they're basically best friends. It about broke Billy's heart when I ended things with Will."

"What's he like, your dad?" I asked Zelda.

She looked pensively out of the window as we drove down the street. "Everyone in town knows Billy Brewer. He's just like Will, a mischievous boy trapped inside a man's body. For all his misgivings Will is actually pretty smart, even if he acts stupid as heck most of the time."

"Was he a good dad to you?" I asked.

Zelda made a face as she considered the question. "Billy was always there for me, but he was also really kind of lousy at being a dad. He wasn't a bad dad, just… not a very good one. Maw Maw was the one that raised me really."

"How come you didn't turn out like her then?" I asked. Nana Bucktooth, big trouble in a small package.

"She was raising me to be the brains of the operation. The Brewer family has always had plenty of muscle, the only problem is they couldn't organize a two-car funeral. Maw Maw is the brains behind everything, that's probably why she refuses to die—everything would go to pot."

"So, you were meant to be her replacement?" I said in amazement.

"Yeah, and I guess I still am. I don't think I'm interested in taking over the business though. This town… it brings out the bad side in me."

After seeing Zelda shakedown that bartender I was inclined to agree.

CHAPTER 16

The 'Hackerty Farm' looked like the type of place you'd find on a picture-perfect postcard. A large farmhouse surrounded by sprawling fields, and several large barns beyond too.

"Wow," I said as we pulled up outside the farmhouse. "I thought you said we were dealing with hillbillies?"

"Just because they're rich don't mean they aren't stupid," Zelda said as she got out of the van. "Besides, this place wasn't this tidy last time I was around here."

"This Will hasn't got any attractive single brothers, has he?" I took a sip of a soda we'd stopped to get along the way.

"It's just Will and his younger brother, Derry. I think Derry just turned twenty."

"Hey, that's not too young for me. He handsome?"

"Handsome, sure. Worst part is that they both know it too. But something tells me you wouldn't be Derry's type." Zelda walked towards the front porch of the house, and I followed her.

"Why not?" I frowned.

"Let's just say that Derry prefers his women with a little more penis." I was halfway through my soda when Zelda decided to drop that one, and I ended up spitting my drink all over myself. Zelda burst out in laughter. "Thought that one might get you."

"How am I related to you?" I wondered out loud.

Zelda knocked on the door and a moment later it swung open. On the other side of the screen door there was a beautiful looking bearded man in a cowboy getup. Now was this Zelda's ex, Will, or his gay brother?

"Well slap my face and call me Mariah Carey, Zelly Brewer!"

I guess that settles that one then.

Derry heaved open the screen door and threw his arms around Zelda, who returned the hug with equal affection. "Girl, look at you! You gone dressed to the nines!" he remarked, his hands on her shoulders as he stepped back. "That brother of mine really must have pissed you off this time!" Derry looked over at me and his smile grew even wider. "Bless my cotton socks I must have mixed up my lemonade with the gin, I'm seeing double."

"Derry this is my sister Zora, she moved to town recently," Zelda explained.

"Out of the way Zelly, you're old news!" Derry playfully pushed Zelda out of the way and came over to kiss the air on either side of my face. "I've heard about you, the detective baker! I am living for *all, of, that*," he said and clapped his hands.

"Thank you, I think?" I said with a confused smile.

"Y'all girls want lemonade? Just whipped up a fresh batch," Derry offered.

"We're here on family business. Where's Will?" Zelda asked, her familiarity fading a little as our focus returned to the task at hand.

"What's he done now?" Derry said and shook his head.

"You probably already know, so you might as well stop pretending," Zelda said reproachfully.

"Who me?" Derry looked offended by the suggestion. "Zelly I'll have you know that Will and I have cleaned up. We ain't criminals no more, we're on the straight and narrow."

"If that's anything like your straight and narrow we have reason to be concerned," I said to Zelda.

"Shut up!" she hissed, punching my arm.

"So, you've seen Zelda's wild streak, huh?" Derry laughed. "I'd heard she'd tried to go all city girl. Can't tame that Brewer in you though, can you?"

Zelda rolled her eyes. "Just tell me where Will is, I know he's the one that's been stealing the Moon Juice."

Derry's laughter stopped all of a sudden and he let out a long whistle. "Well, I ain't going to lie to you. I'm guessing it was that detective sister of yours that helped figure that one out?"

"I'd say it was a team effort."

"What's he doing with it?" Zelda pressed.

"God's honest truth I don't know, and I don't know where he's put it either. I just heard a rumor is all. Will said he only did it as one last favor to your dad. Wound me up to hear about it too. I've been out of town for a few weeks, only got back last night."

"My dad? What's he got to do with this?"

Derry shrugged. "I already told you I don't know that much. I'm out of the game now. I thought Will was out too until I heard about this foolishness. I did ask him about it, but you know how he is, all strong and silent type. I was surprised, we've both had our noses out of the dirt for over a year now."

Zelda looked surprised to hear that. "Wait, seriously?" she asked. "What's going on? You both closing in on your third felony?"

Derry laughed. "Nope, we just decided it was time to clean up our acts, and guess what? We've been making more money ever since we did. We've got a reputation now as well—folks even trust us."

"What is it you do around here?" I asked.

"Horses," Derry said proudly, pointing over to a field full of the beautiful animals. "Breeding, training, you name it—we do it. We even won a couple of awards since we went straight—in business that is, I'm still gayer than a daisy."

Zelda looked at Derry like he was an alien. "I missed your goofy butt."

"Same here, sis," he said, throwing an arm around Zelda and

hugging her again. "You might have left Will in the dust, but I'm still holding out hope. He's changed you know, for real."

"Yeah, stealing from his place of work really suggests he's grown up," Zelda said. "Do you know when he's back? I don't want to confront him at the plant, I'll only end up bumping into everyone else, and then it'll be a whole big thing."

"He's not even over there today, he went fishing with Billy. I'd expect them back in the next few hours or so. You want to come in and take the weight off? I can fix up some lunch if you're hankering."

"Zelda's always hankering," I pointed out.

"Says the one," she fired back at me before looking at Derry. "We'll come in but let me hide the truck first. I want to take them idiots by surprise."

"Oh, they're gonna be surprised alright," Derry exclaimed with a look of glee. "I'm tempted to set up the video recorder to capture the look on their faces!"

* * *

WE WERE WAITING at Derry's house for quite some time. In fact, by the time Will ended up coming back it had grown dark outside and his headlights cutting across the darkness was signal that they were back.

Zelda, Derry and I were waiting in the living room when Will Hackerty and Billy Brewer came through the front door. They were hauling a huge icebox—presumably full of fish—and their fishing gear. Will was just as good looking as his brother, with dark brown eyes and an honest-looking face, which was amusing given his reputation. Billy, Zelda's father, looked a little rougher around the edges, with several days of beard growth on his face, dark circles under his eyes, and an old baseball cap covering a mop of greasy hair.

As soon as they came in, they both stopped dead in their tracks and set their things down.

"Zelda?" Will gasped as though looking at a ghost. He straightened up and started brushing down his shirt.

"Will. Billy," Zelda said, nodding at the both of them. Billy walked forward slowly across the room, put an arm around Zelda and gave her a kiss on the forehead.

"Zelly, it's good to see you, but why do I get the feeling we're in trouble?" Billy said as he pulled out a cigarette.

"No smoking in here anymore, I already told you that," Derry warned him. Billy rolled his eyes and tucked the unlit cigarette into his shirt pocket.

"What are you doing here?" Will asked Zelda, still looking shocked. "I thought you said you were never coming back."

"Well, I think we all knew the chances of that happening were next to slim. Maw Maw practically grabbed me by the scruff of my neck and yanked me back here." She looked over at me and nodded. "This here is Zora." Zelda looked at her father, Billy Brewer. "She's my sister. Momma had her with another man before she had me."

"Yeah, I heard as much," Billy said, chewing at a toothpick. "They say you've been causing trouble across town." He chuckled. "You appear to take after your mother—whether you're as crazy is to be determined."

"Oh, I've got crazy in spades," I said.

"Then you'll fit right in here," Billy laughed.

"I'm guessing you didn't just show up out of the blue to introduce your sister," Will said as he put his things down on the kitchen counter. "Why don't we have a drink? The energy in here is all weird. There's some ice that needs breaking."

"We've already had a drink," Zelda said curtly. "We're here on family business actually. That's why Maw Maw dragged me back here."

Will smiled at her, his dark eyes twinkling dotingly. "You finally came back to take care of the business then, huh? Let me fix you a whisky and we can talk about the—"

"Alright let's cut the crap," Zelda said and pulled out her wand. Without warning she fired a bolt of magic light into the air. It blasted a hole right through the ceiling, raining sawdust and splinters into the room. Everyone jumped into a squat position with their hands up.

"Aw heck Zelly, really?!" Derry said, looking at the hole in the ceiling.

Zelda took no notice of Derry, instead she had her wand pointing straight at her ex-fiancé, Will. "I'm not giving you the chance to use that silver tongue of yours. We're here on business. Someone's been stealing Moon Juice from Maw Maw, and I *know* it was you idiots." Zelda pointed her wand between Will and her dad.

"Zelly you've got the wrong end of the stick," Billy said very casually and started walking towards Zelda. "Put the wand down and we'll talk about this like adults and—" Before he could finish his sentence Zelda blasted another hole in front of Billy Brewer's feet. "Woah now!"

"Zelda!" Derry bellowed. "No more blasting!"

"Sorry Derry," she said, sounding genuinely apologetic. "But you know what these rats are like. Ready to spin words at any opportunity. I thought I'd cut the game short. We've been waiting all day after all."

"Look, Zelly," Will said. "I don't know what's happened to that Moon Juice, but it had nothing to do with us—"

"I *will* blast another hole if you keep lying," Zelda said and pulled out the pool chalk we'd found. "This was up in the old salt sheds, the same place you hid the Moon Juice after you stole it."

Billy and Will both stared at the chalk for a moment. Billy was the first one to break. "Sweet molasses boy, you might as well have left a note and a picture saying we was there!"

Will rolled his eyes at Billy and looked at Zelda with a pleading look. "Look I admit, we're the ones that took it, but you have to believe me—I'm out the game now. I'm straight, me and Derry ain't doing crime no more!"

"Stealing from your employer sure sounds a lot like crime…" I pointed out.

"I know it looks bad," Will admitted. "But it's his fault." He jerked a thumb at Billy Brewer. "I owed him one and he basically forced me to do it."

Zelda pointed the wand at her dad. "That true?"

Billy let out a very long sigh, pulled the cigarette out his pocket and went to light it again before Derry reprimanded him again. "You light that cigarette Billy Brewer, so help me god."

"Alright, I forgot!" Billy huffed before putting the cigarette back once more. He rubbed his eyes and looked at Zelda. "Will you put the wand down? You've already got our attention."

Zelda considered the request for a moment before doing so. "Fine but start talking."

"In a way this is *your* fault," Billy began. With those words an incensed rage came over Zelda's face, an expression so laden with fury that Billy quickly took the words back. "That's one way of looking at it of course! But not the way I'd call it!"

"Just start talking, *quickly*," Zelda said through her teeth.

"When you left town and broke off the engagement with Will he was a mess," Billy explained.

"Is this necessary?" Will said, glaring at Billy.

Billy threw his hands in the air. "Boy I'm taking the heat here for you, now let me explain why! That fair?" Will looked like it wasn't fair at all, but he gave a slight nod of his head, nonetheless. Billy resumed his story. "After you left town, this idiot took to drinking, in a bad way too. He was out fishing on the lake one night by himself and he took two bottles of Jack for company. They were empty on the bottom of the boat by the time he fell in the water."

Zelda gasped and looked at Will. "You idiot. You could have drowned!"

"Yeah, and I would have if Billy here hadn't pulled me out of the water," Will admitted reluctantly.

Billy straightened his cap. "As luck had it, I was coming back from O'Leary's place on my boat. By complete fluke I came around the corner just as I saw this idiot struggling with his line. I saw him fall in and knew he was drunk out of his mind and not coming back up again. Anyway, I hustled over, dived in and pulled him out. Nearly drowned me trying to get him out."

Derry looked at them both, seemingly perplexed by the story. "You never told me about that," he said to Will.

"Didn't exactly fancy sharing my darkest moment with every damn soul in this town," Will explained. He took a deep breath and looked away. "Anyway, after that I told Billy I owed him one. Anytime he wanted to call it in, I had a favor with his name on it. Anything he wanted, no questions asked." Will looked at Zelda. "I promise you I'm on the straight and narrow now, but Billy cashed that favor in recently. He saved my life Zelly, I'm not about to say no when he needs me."

Zelda looked at Will pitifully, then turned her gaze to her dad. Her expression changed with that slight movement, from understanding to rage. "Let's hear it then, why the heck have you been stealing from Maw Maw?"

Billy blew out air and scratched the back of his head. "It's probably best we just show you," he said, looking at Will for his approval.

"They're only going to find out anyway," Will conceded. "Might as well rip the band aid off. It's in the barn, come on, I'll show you."

"The barn?!" Derry exclaimed. "You're reprising this criminal enterprise in our barn of all places! We're clean now, Will!"

Will looked at his brother as though he understood full well. "Look, I only did this as a favor to Billy. I'm still on the straight and narrow with you, I promise. This is just one small hiccup until Billy finds a better place to put it."

"It?" Zelda asked.

"Just... just come and look," Billy sighed.

The five of us went outside around the back of the farmhouse and followed a small dirt track to a large barn at the back of the property. Will unlocked the doors and threw them open. As the doors swung wide, we saw straight away what it was they were hiding back here.

CHAPTER 17

Standing before us there was a huge bear, so massive that it was easily larger than an elephant. Its coat wasn't dark brown, but a metallic and lustrous gold color that caught the silver moonlight and cast scattered light across the dark barn interior. On its forehead a dark crescent moon shape occurred naturally in the fur, and its large eyes were ink black and full. Warm air came gently from the huge beasts' muzzle, it blinked and shifted across paws the size of tree trunks.

"Oh my god... these fools have a Moon Bear in my barn," Derry said quietly.

"*Small* hiccup?" Zelda said, looking at Will and Billy with her arms crossed.

"I'll admit it's possibly in the realms of a medium hiccup..." Will mumbled.

I had no idea what this magical creature was, but it felt significant and majestic, like I was looking into the eyes of an old god. "What is this thing?" I gasped. "It's beautiful."

"Moon Bear," Zelda explained. "I've never seen one in person before. They're incredibly rare—I didn't even think they were real."

"She's a treasure, isn't she?" Billy said proudly. "I found her out in the woods not long back when I was doing a branching ritual. Had to pinch myself to be sure I wasn't dreaming. She came right on over and plucked a cannister of Moon Juice right off my back. Drank the entire thing straight down."

"She drank the Moon Juice?" I asked in amazement.

Zelda nodded as though it was to be expected. "Moon Juice isn't just a cauldron catalyst; it has another purpose too—magical creatures love to drink it. It's nourishing and something of a sedative." She looked at Billy. "That's why you're stealing the Moon Juice. How many cannisters you getting through to keep her in here? Ten a day? Fifteen?"

"Twenty," Billy corrected. He pointed over to the corner of the barn at a large tarp covering. "The juice is under there. Luna loves her Moon Juice."

Zelda scoffed. "Luna?"

"That's what we called her," Will said. "She's quite placid you know; you can touch her if you want. She likes the attention."

As annoyed as Zelda was, she didn't want to miss out on this rare opportunity. She reached out an unsure hand and placed it on the large bear's muzzle. "She's so warm!" Zelda gasped with delight.

"She's a beauty alright," Billy agreed.

After a moment Zelda pulled her hands away and her disapproval returned. "This might be the stupidest thing either of you has ever done. These creatures are so rare they're basically legendary. You can't keep it locked up in a barn dosed up on Moon Juice!"

"We have a plan," Will said with assurance, "and it's not as black and white as you make it out to be."

"Really?" Zelda said. She looked at me. "Here's a tidbit about Moon Bears, Zora. Every full moon they shed their fur—real gold. All that gold? It drops to the ground for anyone to pick up. Poxy usually get to it first." She turned to Will and Billy. "That's what you're doing here, isn't it? Waiting for this thing to drop its fur so you can farm this animal for money."

"Not exactly. She already dropped her coat," Will said. He walked into the barn over to a stack of what I thought were plastic-wrapped haybales.

"Twice already," Billy corrected.

Will pulled out a pocketknife and made a small slash in the haybale nearest to him. The black wrap split slightly, and a little torrent of golden fur spilled out for a few seconds. He turned and gestured at the wall of haybales. "We cleaned it all up of course."

"We reckon each malting is $50k of gold, easy," Billy said eagerly.

"Sweet mother of Moses," Derry whispered.

"That is a lot of gold…" I commented.

Zelda turned and looked at her father and ex. "That still doesn't change the fact that what you're doing here is wrong. You can't keep an animal like this locked up."

"We agree," Will and Billy both said at the same time. Their mutual agreement took Zelda by surprise.

"Huh?"

"Billy didn't give you the whole story about how he found Luna. When she came to him, she had an ivory spear buried in her chest," Will said.

"Close to dead she was," Billy added. "Someone tried to hunt her, Zelly. We've been keeping her here to nurse her back to health. The maltings are an added bonus, I guess, but that's not what we were keeping her here for, I promise."

It was then that I noticed there was a line in the bear's fur between its front legs, a large white scar that ran from the top of its neck down to where its heart would be.

"You fixed her up?" Zelda asked.

Billy nodded. "Sure did! I know I'm not good for much, but I've always been good at looking at after animals at least."

"That you have," she agreed quietly.

"Why would someone hunt a creature like this?" I asked.

"We've been asking ourselves the same question," Will said as he gave the Moon Bear a scritch on its muzzle. "The only conclusion we can draw is that it has something to do with dark witches."

Zelda and I exchanged a look. "Dark witches?" I said and cleared my throat.

"We did some looking up on it," Billy said. "Apparently the Moon Bear's heart is an ingredient in powerful dark magic rituals. Some sicko out there was trying to core the thing right out of her body."

"You think it's the Sisters of the Shade?" Zelda said to me.

I shrugged. "I don't know. We've not seen them around for a while, but they're obviously still hanging around town." Between flooding Compass Cove with cursed jewelry, trying to abduct me and now this… what were they up to?

"The Sisters of the Shade are back?" Billy Brewer exclaimed with a long whistle. "Boy I thought we'd seen the back of those broads. I'd definitely put them up to something like this."

"It seems they're having a resurgence," Zelda said. "They attacked Zora not long back." She looked at me. "What do you think we do here?"

"Me?" I asked in bewilderment. "What do I have to do with this?"

"Well, you're a prismatic witch, you basically outrank everyone when it comes to stuff like this."

"Zelda, I magicked up a rhino a few days ago when I tried to conjure a teacup, I'm hardly an authority on matters like this," I pointed out.

"That was your wand, not you," she argued.

"If you really are a prismatic witch then Zora is right," Will agreed. "Your powers will give you an ability to communicate through Luna, maybe even see through her eyes and give us a glimpse of who attacked her. Put your hand on her muzzle and see what happens. One thing is for certain, we can't let her out into the woods until we know her attackers are gone."

I realized then that everyone was looking at me in expectation. It was a strange sensation constantly feeling like I was the most important person in a room when I knew next to nothing about magic—I knew for sure that everyone here had more magical knowledge than me, but when it came down to things, they were always convinced my innate abilities would trump their experience. I still didn't feel totally on board with that idea.

"Fine," I huffed, lifting my hand up to touch Luna's muzzle. "But it's not like anything is going to—happen!"

But something *did* happen. As soon as I placed my hand on the huge bear's snout it was like a giant hand picked me up and pulled me into the air, the world around me shrinking down a long tunnel. Everything went black and when I opened my eyes again, I was in the woods, sniffing at dead leaves on the ground.

I then realized that I wasn't me, I was inside the Moon Bear's head, reliving one of its earlier memories:

My huge paws dug through soft soil and then I caught the scent of something delicious on the air. Honey.

I bounded towards a nearby tree and sure enough there was a beehive hanging from one of its high branches. I pounced up and put a paw on the branch, which shattered immediately under my huge weight. As the branch crashed to the floor so did the beehive. I dropped down, scooped up the hive in my mouth and bit down. Delicious honey oozed across my tongue and scores of little bees tried to sting me.

After devouring the delicious beehive, I wondered on through the forest, looking for more things to eat. I found some nice berries and caught the scent of rushing water further downhill; that would be a nice place to catch some fish.

It was just as I turned in that direction that I saw something blur past my vision, followed by a loud clatter. I turned to follow the sound and saw a long white thing buried in the tree—a spear.

Then there came another blur, and I saw a figure standing about twenty feet away from me, a human with a dark cloak over their face. The human pulled back their arm and launched another long white spear, this one burying deep into my front.

Without understanding why they were attacking me I bounded towards them and knocked them over. I didn't stop after that, I kept running until I was sure I lost my attacker.

Then I saw another human, a man standing over a fire. There was something calming about his energy, and I knew that I could trust him.

"Oh my goodness..." he said as he saw me come out of the trees. "Is that a... okay girl, easy now!"

I approached a shiny box with some sort of delicious scent inside. Somewhat like a beehive, but different. Picking it up in my mouth I tilted my head back and let my teeth puncture the hard exterior.

"So, you like Moon Juice?" the man chuckled and placed a calming hand on my side. "That figures. My goodness, who did this to you?" he gasped. "Looks like someone's been hunting you." He paused and looked around for any sign of the attacker. "This wound needs healing fast. Do you like the juice? Do you want more?"

More? I'd love more. There's more of this stuff? Take me to it!

"Come on, follow me," the friendly man said. "There's plenty more where that came from."

THE EXPERIENCE ENDED ALMOST AS QUICKLY as it began, and when I snapped out of it, I felt myself falling back down the long tunnel that plucked me from the ground in the first place. I landed back in my body with what felt like a bang and pulled my hand away from the huge bear's muzzle. Without meaning to I stumbled back and landed butt-first on the ground.

"Zora? Are you okay?" Zelda said, rushing to help me back to my feet.

"I'm fine," I said, realizing I was out of breath. "I don't know what happened. It's like I was in the bear's head. I saw it getting attacked, and I saw it find you Billy."

"What did they look like?" Billy asked. "The attacker?"

"I didn't get a clear look at their face, but it was a witch in a hooded robe."

"Sure sounds like the Sisters of the Shade alright," Will said. "Man, I can't believe they're really back."

"Back and up to their old tricks." Billy turned and spit on the ground.

"Look, I fully support y'all taking in injured animals and all," Derry said, "but I think this thing is outside of your remit, even for your Billy."

"Yeah, we were just having that conversation out on the lake," Billy admitted. "But I don't know what to do with her. We can't release her back out into the wild until we catch those hunters but keeping her here long term ain't going to work either. I know her coat looks dazzling, but you should have seen how bright it was when we first brought her in. I've never seen anything quite like it."

Will nodded his head in agreement. "Her coat is growing back duller with each malting. She's not meant to be cooped up inside like this, she needs the freedom of the forest. Until we catch those hunters I don't know what do to though—it's not like there are folk that specialize in taking care of rare magical animals like this."

For a moment I found myself mindlessly agreeing, but then it occurred to me: I might know just the person that could help. "Actually, I think I know someone that might be able to look after her."

Both Will and Billy looked at me. "Really, who?" Will asked.

"His name is Hudson, he works for an agency that specializes in this type of thing, and by that, I mean looking after wild magical animals. Compass Cove is actually his territory."

The duo both appeared unsure about the idea. "I don't know," Billy said with uncertainty. "How do we know we can trust him? I don't want Luna going to just anyone."

"Hudson is the real deal, dad," Zelda said. "I've seen him work. He knows more about magical animals than just about any person I've met."

"When can he come and check her out?" Will asked.

"I'll give him a call now and see if he can come over."

"He's never far away from Zora..." Zelda said with a smirk.

Sure enough when I called Hudson he said he'd come straight on over. I gave him the address and twenty minutes later he and Blake arrived in Blake's cruiser.

"What's with the cowgirl getup?" Hudson said to me with amusement as he got out the car.

"You know what they say. When in Rome." Derry and I brought them to the barn and they both went wide-eyed upon seeing the Moon Bear.

"Holy crap," Blake gawped. "I thought these things were mythical."

Hudson looked shocked too, though not as much. "Wow, I've got to admit I wasn't expecting an actual Moon Bear. These things are a rare sight, even for me."

"See, see—I don't like this," Billy said. "Even the magic animal man doesn't know them!"

"Oh, I know them alright," Hudson said calmly. "See the crest on her forehead there? It shouldn't be that dark. She's overdue a long sleep. Moon Bears typically sleep for three months and rise briefly to feed. That's why her coat's looking so dim—you're tired, aren't you girl?"

"What are our options?" I said to Hudson. "They don't want to let her back in the woods because the hunter is still out there, but they can't keep her pent up here either."

He shook his head in understanding. "No, she can't stay here too much longer. Without a long sleep she'll start firing quills and Moon Bears can breathe radiant fire too."

Will Hackerty and Billy Brewer laughed. "She can't breathe fire!" Billy said.

"Yeah... no quills either," Will added.

Hudson moved his hand gently under Luna's throat and squeezed lightly. In response the bear lifted its head and let out a ray of brilliant white fire. "Fire," he said calmly. "And..." Moving his hand up behind the bear's jaw he applied pressure and a crown of black quills appeared around the top of Luna's head. "Quills!"

"Okay..." Will said slowly. "Maybe this guy does a know his stuff."

"I'll double check with HQ, but I think we've got the perfect place to keep her safe until this hunter is apprehended," Hudson said to Will and Billy. "We've got acres of private woodland where she can run free in perfect safety."

"Heck, sounds good to me," Will said. "Billy, what do you think?"

Billy looked personally tortured by the suggestion. "You promise you'll keep her safe?" he asked Hudson.

"I swear on it," Hudson said, holding out his hand. After a moment of reluctance Billy shook his hand, followed by Will.

"Well, that's settled then," Blake said, clapping his hands together lightly.

"And that means our business with Nana Bucktooth is settled. We should go tell her the good news." I glanced at Hudson and Blake. "We can even get your curse broken."

Zelda looked horrified by the suggestion. "Oh no, it'll have to wait until tomorrow. It's after eight in the evening now. You never bother Maw Maw after eight."

"What?" I laughed. "Why?"

"Trust Zelly on this one," Derry said. "After eight is Nana Bucktooth's Jeopardy time."

"And god forbid any poor soul that interrupts Jeopardy time," Billy added.

"I made the sorry mistake of doing that once," Will said with a shudder. "Never again."

"Uh… okay, I'll take your word for it. Blake, Hudson, hopefully you guys can go one more day with this curse?"

"Eh," Blake shrugged. "At this point I'm used to lugging this idiot around everywhere I go."

Hudson mirrored the sentiment. "I'm sure we can go one more day without killing each other… probably."

CHAPTER 18

Seeing as I was fixing things left, right, and center, I decided to try and put some attention towards the biggest problem currently haunting my life: clearing Daphne's name of murder. The next morning I woke up early to help Rosie and Daphne with the day's bake, and I also took a little time to study the books and see how things had been going since taking Rosie on.

The answer? Pretty terrific actually.

"Wait a second. You've set three consecutive record days since working here," I said to Rosie in amazement. I was in the kitchen entering numbers into spreadsheets while the girls finished up details on the bake.

"What can I tell you, boss? Rosie said with her Irish lilt. "Mother always said I've got the gift of the gab."

"That's an understatement. You should see her with the customers, Zora," Daphne said. "If Rosie opened up her own bakery we'd be out of business in a month."

"Don't go giving her any ideas," I gulped. "I reckon you might be right."

"Now there's an idea!" Rosie sang while piping some eclairs. "Rosie

O'Brian with her own business. I think my father would weep! Owning a business isn't for me though. Paying taxes and filing paperwork. That's not what Rosie likes to do."

"Still, you have to file your own taxes at the end of the year," Daphne pointed out.

Rosie blew air out of her lips. "Nope, I don't do that. I think the government already has enough money; they don't need my paltry contributions."

"But—but you could get arrested!" Daphne said, wide-eyed.

Rosie just grinned darkly. "I'd like to see them yellow bellies try."

"Well, if you could try and avoid jail for a few months at least—this summer will be fabulous if we've got you on our team. If you're planning any shootouts with federal agents at least wait until the winter season when things quiet down."

"Aye, aye, captain," Rosie said in mock salute. "I won't kill any more police before winter!"

"What does she mean by 'any more?'" Daphne whispered to me quietly.

"I don't know, but I'm not sticking around to find out," I said and shut the laptop, before hurrying out of the kitchen and up the stairs to my apartment. "The less I know the better!" I had this feeling that my chances of being an accessory to a crime got higher by the minute when I was in a room with Rosie.

Not long after that I said goodbye to the girls and went outside to get picked up by Blake and Hudson. When we left Wildwood last night, we'd arranged to meet up outside the bakery just after ten. As soon as I stepped onto the sidewalk Blake's cruiser came around the corner and he pulled up. I climbed inside the car and buckled up. I at least expected a hello, but no, they carried on with a conversation that had clearly been building for some time.

"You're missing the point entirely," Blake said. "If every character in Harry Potter fought the entirety of the United States Army, it wouldn't even be close. Magic trumps guns, *fact*."

Hudson, who had his head cradled in one hand as he looked out the window, just blew air out of his nose and laughed. "Take it from someone that is *literally* enhanced with magic. You're talking out of your ass."

Once upon a time that kind of comment would have resulted in a full-blown fist fight between the two of them, but to my surprise Blake just laughed even harder. "Hudson, just think about it. A wizard could take on fifty soldiers *easy*. Voldemort against a platoon of men with guns? Blood bath!"

Hudson chuckled. "Yeah, the big bad guy? Sure? But what about one of the bajillion characters that aren't extremely powerful wizards? Neville Longbottom against an M4 Carbine? His brains are all over the floor before he can open his mouth to squeak Latin. Don't even get me started on nukes. Hogwarts might have magic defenses, but it'd be left in the dust after a 1.2 megaton nuclear bomb. By the way, I've not even mentioned how *few* magic people there are in the wizard population in Harry Potter. We're talking a couple thousand against a couple hundred thousand, it's not even close, in fact—"

"Good morning!" I said from the back of the car, wondering how much longer this conversation was going to go on for. They both turned around in surprise, like they hadn't even seen or heard me enter the car.

"Zora, how long have you been here!" Blake said in surprise.

"I got in the car literally the moment you pulled up."

"Sorry, we had a pretty important debate to get straight," Hudson said. "Maybe you could chip in, who would—"

"Maybe I could go and do this mystery business by myself," I thought out loud. "I'd probably get it done in half the time."

"Alright, alright," Blake laughed. "We get the message. How are you doing?"

"I'm great, how's the case going? I assume you *have* been working it, and not just having these arguments for the last few days."

"We've been trying," Hudson said. "Trying to get hold of these other two suspects though hasn't been easy. It's like trying to catch smoke."

"Who are we trying to track down?" I asked.

"Mitchell Murphy, one of Black's old songwriting partners, and Molly Gould, Black's ex-fiancé. Both of them are like shadows in the night. We can't find any record of Murphy anywhere, and Molly Gould is apparently staying with one of her boyfriends, but we haven't been able to track her down either."

"Have you looked for Mitchell Murphy using his real name?" I asked.

Blake and Hudson looked at one another for a moment before looking back at me. "What do you mean, real name?" Blake asked.

"Mitchell Murphy's real name is Gavin Price," I said. "Mitchell Murphy is a stage name he coined when he and Black started *Midnight Crow Explosion*. I saw it in a documentary about the band a few years ago."

"Wait, you actually liked this band?" Blake said in amazement.

"They have good songs! Don't judge me! Anyway, Murphy quickly realized the stage wasn't for him, so he moved offstage to be the band's main songwriter. All the biggest songs on the first album came from him, then he left the band, and every album after that written by Black. That's when the real hits started."

Hudson's gaze lingered a moment before he shook his head and looked back at Blake. "What's your computer say? Anything on Gavin Price?"

"Just looking it up now," Blake said as he slowly pecked away at a keyboard with his fingers. "Stupid thing, still doesn't make any sense to me."

"Give that here," Hudson said, snatching the keyboard off Blake. I guess I hadn't realized it before, but Blake and technology didn't exactly get on. Hudson's fingers blurred over the keyboard, and something came up on the screen. "Ah, ha! There he is!"

"What is it?" I asked.

"Gavin Price, Montezuma Heights." Hudson let out a long whistle. "That's pricey real estate. Those big looking glass apartments by the waterfront? Says here he has the penthouse."

Blake started the engine and even put the siren on. "I say we go and pay him a visit then. Now Zora, before we get there can I ask you an important question?" he said and pulled out into the road.

"Throw it at me," I said keenly.

"One fighter jet against a Hippogriff, the Hippogriff wins nine times out of ten, right?"

"Let me out of this car right now," I groaned.

* * *

BLAKE LET OUT a long whistle as we got out of the car. "Wow, I should really go into songwriting, obviously I'm in the wrong business."

Hudson smirked. "I've heard your singing, I think you should definitely stay out of the music game."

Blake tilted his head in consideration. "That's probably fair."

Montezuma heights was a ten-story glass front building that overlooked Compass Cove Harbor. It was high-end real estate for people that obviously had a lot of cash to burn.

"How much does a place like this go for?" I asked as we approached the lobby doors.

"I checked it up on the way here," Hudson said. "A couple of million, easily."

"Looks like this guy made a good chunk even if he left the band early on," Blake commented.

We buzzed the penthouse and a moment later a man's voice came over the speaker. "Hello?"

"Good morning, I'm Officer Blake Voss, here with my associates Hudson Beck and Zora Wick. We're investigating Patrick Black's murder and hoping we could ask Gavin Price a few questions."

A moment of breathy hesitation crackled down the speaker. "... Come on in then."

The doors opened and we took the elevator up to the penthouse. When we reached the floor the doors opened straight into the apartment, Gavin Price, who I knew better as Mitchell Murphy, was waiting for us by the entrance. He had a skinny frame and was on the shorter side, with pale skin, thinning hair and a weak jaw.

"Tea? Coffee?" he asked as we came into the foyer of his penthouse.

"No, we're good thanks. We just want to talk," I said.

"Are you sure? I just got a $20,000 espresso machine plumbed in. Best coffee you'll ever have, I guarantee it."

"Uh... sure then, go ahead," Blake conceded.

"Kitchen is through here, follow me," Mitchell said.

We followed Mitchell into the kitchen, which was part of a wide open-space apartment that looked like it came out of a high-end design magazine. Mitchell went straight over to a long chrome machine that looked like it belonged in a small café, not a domestic kitchen.

"So, Mr. Price," Hudson began.

"Actually, you can call me Mitchell, Mitchel Murphy," he corrected. "I've not gone by that other name for a long time."

"Isn't the apartment registered in that name?" Blake asked.

"Yes," Mitchell said as he poured some coffee beans into a tall black machine. "I still use it for anonymity's sake. Even though I left the band years ago I still get a lot of attention." Mitchell pressed a button on the black machine and a loud mechanical grinding noise filled the kitchen. We waited until it was over to resume the conversation.

"We understand you were at the mansion the day Black died," I continued. "After talking with a few different people your name kept coming up as someone we should speak to."

Murphy scoffed, and rolled his eyes, but kept on preparing our drinks. I watched in fascination as he moved mindlessly through the routine, one that he looked very familiar with. "Yeah, a lot of people in Black's camp still have it in for me. I guess you could say thing's didn't end well between us."

"It looks like you made out alright," Blake noted, gesturing to the luxury apartment surrounding us.

"It might seem that way, but in wake of what I could have had, this is a consolation prize—let me assure you," Mitchell said as he filled a metal pitcher with milk and started steaming it.

"A luxury waterfront penthouse and a $20,000 espresso machine," Hudson commented, "That's one hell of a consolation prize."

"Let me ask *you* a question," Mitchell said. "Do you know how much money *Midnight Crow Explosion* has made since its inception? I'll spare you the guessing... it's north of 40 million dollars."

"Alright, we definitely chose the wrong job," Hudson said to Blake.

"My knowledge of the band's history is a little fuzzy," Blake said, "but from my understanding you were only part of the band from the first album, is that correct?"

"That's... correct," Mitchell said and handed Blake and Hudson a latte each.

"And after that Patrick Black was credited as the sole songwriter for the remaining albums?" I followed.

"Yes." Murphy's lips were pressed tight together, he handed me a drink too, a latte with a delicately poured tulip on top. I took a sip of the drink and had to do a double take. "Man, you weren't kidding about the coffee, it's great!"

Hudson looked impressed too, but Blake's face portrayed dissatisfaction. "Not to your taste?" Murphy asked.

"I think I'm too used to drinking it my way—cheap and cheerful." Blake set the cup down. "So, help me understand something. I sense resentment from you about the way things ended with Black, but it seems to me you've been more than compensated for your short time with the band. Is that an accurate assessment of the situation?"

Murphy put his own drink down and let out a very long breath. "I suppose I'm allowed to tell you the truth as you're law enforcement. When I left the band, I signed a legal agreement saying I'd never talk about this out in public. Now that Black is dead it doesn't really matter as much—regardless, this information shouldn't really leave this room."

We all leaned in close at that moment, intrigued to hear what Murphy had to say. "Go on," I said keenly.

"Black never wrote a song for the band. It was all me. The first album was entirely my construction, and every album after that came from songs that I wrote in the band's first two years. The truth is that

Black stole my songwriting book, kicked me out of the band and took credit for my work. He got the mansions and the fat checks, and I had to settle out of court for a measly 3% of everything the band earned. I had no way of proving the work he stole was mine, he really had me bent over a barrel. The studio took his side because he was the front man—they said his 'image' sold the music."

Blake and Hudson seemed moderately surprised by the revelation, but as an actual fan of the band's music my jaw was nearly on the floor. "Is that why the last album was so bad?" I asked. After half a dozen killer albums the latest release from Black's band was, to put it lightly, abysmal.

Murphy smiled knowingly and nodded. "Yup, Black finally used up all the songs that he stole from me. I must admit it was satisfying to hear just how poor *his* abilities were, though of course I always knew that." He grabbed a box of cigarettes off the counter and then searched his pockets, presumably for a lighter.

We all watched as he pulled out a variety of the most random items. There was a tape measure, a large spring, a ball of elastic bands, a folded-up instruction manual from Monopoly, and finally a lighter. It was like watching MacGyver empty out his pockets.

"Uh, quite the collection of items you have there," I noted.

He chuckled. "I have this habit of putting things in my pockets without noticing." Murphy paused to light his cigarette, pulled his empty cup a little closer and tapped ash into it.

"Where were we?" Blake said, steering things back on track.

"Some would say you had a pretty just reason to want Black dead then," Hudson surmised.

"Yeah, I can see how it looks that way. I've had a lot of years and a lot of chances to get back at him though—why would I leave it until now?" Murphy huffed.

"How come you were at the party if you hated him so much? Why would Black invite you?" Blake asked.

"I don't know why he invited me actually. When I received the invite I threw it in the trash, but then my curiosity got the better of me. I heard rumors that Patrick had a proposal for me, but I never actually got a chance to talk with him at the party—so I guess we'll never know."

"Maybe he wanted more songs?" I hazarded.

"Maybe. Like I said, someone killed the sucker before we got to talk, so it's a mystery."

"This is quite the kitchen you've got here," I said, regarding the arrangement of glistening countertops and expensive appliances. It rivaled my own professional setup. "Do you do a lot of cooking?"

"Not really," Murphy answered. "This is my girlfriend's domain, half of my money goes into here, but I couldn't tell you what half of this stuff does."

"I had a girlfriend like that once," Blake said familiarly. "Emphasis on *had*."

Murphy chuckled politely. "Yes, well… are we done here then? I *do* have things to do today."

"Where is she now?" Hudson asked, glossing over Murphy's attempt to end the questioning.

"Uh, yoga class I think," Murphy said. "She's been out since this morning, won't be back until later today."

"What's she proofing in that bowl over there?" I asked Murphy, nodding to a bowl of dough on the counter behind him.

"Huh?" he asked, turning to regard the bowl. "Oh, I'm not sure actually. I think she's making bread."

"That dough is going to be seriously over-proofed by the time she gets back," I said with a smile.

Murphy looked at me curiously. "I'll have to take your word for it. She can be quite forgetful."

"One last question—" I said, finishing the last of my coffee and setting it down on the counter. As I did so I accidentally placed the cup down too forcefully. The porcelain shattered and I drew my hand back quickly, realizing that I had sliced my thumb open. "Ah!"

Blake and Hudson were on their feet immediately, dramatic response as usual. "Zora!" Blake said with concern.

"I'm fine, it's just a small nick, sorry about the cup," I said and looked at Murphy. He had a hand over his mouth and taken a step back. "Uh... is everything okay?"

"It's okay... sorry. I'm just a little queasy around blood." Murphy cautiously handed me some kitchen roll and I applied pressure to the wound. "Please excuse me for a moment, I feel a little nauseous," he said. Murphy walked out of the kitchen, and I heard a door closing somewhere in the apartment.

"Is this a scheme, or a genuine accident?" Hudson asked.

"Accident," I said. Blake came around the counter and helped clean up the mess.

"Still, it looks like he's not a fan of blood," Blake observed. "You saw how that crime scene was—I don't think Murphy could do that—not after how he just reacted."

"Maybe," I said with slow consideration. An idea came to mind then. "Wait here!"

Without offering an explanation I quickly retraced Black's footsteps to a closed door between the apartment and the elevator doors. I heard a flush on the other side of the door, stepped back and waited for the door to open before I deliberately walked into Murphy.

"Entschuldigung!" I said quickly, stepping back after stumbling into him.

"Quite alright," Murphy responded, looking a little surprised and confused about the unexpected collision. He carried on back in the direction of the kitchen and I went into the bathroom, closing the door behind me.

When I came back to the kitchen, I found that Blake and Hudson had tried to sucker Murphy into their earlier argument. "Honestly, I've never read the books, so I couldn't say..." Mitchell said.

"But it's not about the books really," Blake began. "It's about magic versus—"

"I think we're done here," I said as I came into the kitchen. "Come on, let's hit the road. Mister Murphy we'll be back in touch if we need anything else, is that okay?"

"Certainly," Mitchell said with a nod of his head. "I'm always happy to help."

Together the three of us took the elevator back to the lobby and walked to the car. "What was that about?" Blake asked once we were clear of the apartment. "Where did you disappear to in such a hurry?"

"I bumped into him on purpose as he was coming out of the bathroom."

Blake and Hudson looked perplexed. "Why on earth did you do that?" Hudson questioned. As way of demonstration, I body checked him and bounced off his impervious weight.

"Entschuldigung!" I repeated.

"What did you just say? Was that some kind of spell?" he asked.

"I think she might be having a stroke," Blake answered.

"You know for two guys that claim to have German heritage you're really letting the side down. It means 'sorry' in German. I said it as soon as I bumped into Mitchell Murphy, and he understood it perfectly."

"Yeah, he also nearly fainted when you cut your hand open too," Blake pointed out. "If speaking German is an admission of guilt we might as well lock you up."

"The guy said he doesn't know his way around the kitchen either," Hudson said. "I have a feeling he's not our man, Zora."

I shrugged and climbed into the back seat of the cruiser. "You know what, you may very well be right. Now who's our next suspect?"

"Molly Gould," Blake said and started the engine. "But it's like looking for a needle in a haystack."

"She's one of those influencers, right?" I asked.

Hudson nodded. "Yeah, something like that, why?"

"Give me your phone. I know how to find her."

With an air of regret Hudson passed the phone over to me. "You've got that weird look in your eye. What are you planning?"

"I'm going fishing, Hudson," I said and held up his phone. "This is my rod, now I've just got to think up some bait." I opened up the app, found Molly Gould's profile and set my brain into motion.

"Well, I vote we get lunch on the way," Blake said. "I'm starving."

"Now *that* I agree with," Hudson cheered.

"Another vote from me," I said as my fingers tapped over the phone's keyboard. "Say, how much do you know about cryptocurrency?" I asked Hudson.

"Uh, next to nothing, why?" he laughed.

"Because you're my bait, and I know just how to get Molly Gould out of hiding."

CHAPTER 19

By the time we finished eating, my trap had been set and Molly Gould had responded—just as I intended.

"Zora, I just don't understand how any of this stuff works," Hudson groaned. "I can't pretend I'm some guru that wants her to promote some new internet currency!"

"Why not?" I asked. "I seriously doubt she understands half of this stuff either. Look at her profile, half of the posts on there she's shilling one of these random crypto coins. Every video is the same, she just follows a script and gets paid her fee." To demonstrate I held up one of the videos and let it play.

"*Hey guys Molly here! Today I'm super excited to tell you about a new opportunity. This is a chance to get in on the ground floor and make some serious money! If you use the promo code MGOULD20 you'll even get 20 extra tokens completely for free! Go to...*"

"See? It's not complicated," I said and swiped the video closed.

"Let me get this straight," Blake said as he stared at the phone. "There is money *inside* the phone?"

Hudson shook his head at Blake. "I understand it more than him at least."

"Look, she's already taken the bait," I said, turning the phone around to show him the conversation. I'd set up a fake profile using Hudson's pictures, claiming that he was a 'Crypto Expert' with a new an upcoming coin. Before eating lunch, I'd sent this message to Molly Gould's profile:

Hey Miss Gould, my name is Hudson and I represent a new and exciting cryptocurrency called Rainbow Dawg. We're interested in having you promote this thrilling new opportunity and are curious as to what your fees are? I'm local to Compass Cove if you'd like to meet up and discuss it.

She responded with:

Hey supes grateful and excited for the op. My fee is $10,000 per post. I can meet today x

"Holy heck!" Blake remarked. "Ten thousand dollars for one post!" He looked at Hudson. "Scrap the songwriting career, we're going to be influencers."

Hudson chuckled. "Coming from the guy that can't use a calculator." He turned his attention to me. "Okay I'll give it to you; this is a pretty genius plan."

"Thank you, and once we have her in public it's not like we actually have to follow up on this stuff. It's just a ruse to get her out of hiding." I tapped another message on the phone, asking her where a good place was to meet up. Almost straightaway she responded:

La Font restaurant on Main Street. I'll be there all day.

With a grin I held up the message so Hudson and Blake could see it. "Looks like we've got a location, boys."

They both looked impressed. Blake clapped his hands and stood up. "Let's go then team. Time to upload a new internet money to the mainframe and become meme millionaires." He looked at me. "That's close, right?"

"Not even in the same ballpark," I said.

Hudson clasped a hand on his shoulder. "I'd stick with the songwriting pal, and that's saying something."

* * *

I'D WALKED past *La Font* restaurant a few times before, but I'd never actually been inside. Speaking truthfully the place looked very upmarket, a little above the kind of joint that I liked to go to. Zelda often said I reminded her of a wild animal whenever I was eating, and I didn't think that kind of vibe would sit well in a place like this.

As it was the middle of the day the restaurant was naturally closed, but the front doors were open so we walked straight in. Inside it was quiet, but we heard voices coming from the kitchen, so we carried on through to the back.

There we found a large man in a chef's apron, accompanied by none other than Molly Gould. She was an immaculate blonde barbie type, not a single hair out of place.

"Am sorry, we are closed—" the man said in a heavy French accent. He and Molly were both working at a counter, rows of elaborate little patisserie creations in front of them.

"Oh wait, Jacques, I think these are the people that just messaged me." Molly straightened up, dusted off her hands and looked at Hudson with familiarity. "You're the crypto guy, right?"

"Actually no, I'm afraid not. My name is Hudson Beck, this if Officer Blake Voss and this here is my associate, Zora Wick. We're here to ask you a few questions about Patrick Black's murder."

Molly's smile dropped and she stared at us for a few seconds before responding. "Oh... fudge."

Her large French chef companion didn't stop what he was doing— piping delicate little cakes with picture perfect frosted flowers. "I told you they would come; you might as well talk to them."

The elusive suspect sank back into her chair and crossed her arms, scowling at us like an upset child. "I suppose we should get this over with then," she huffed.

Blake took a seat at the counter, but Hudson and I remained standing. Straightaway I noticed something of interest on the counter—a metal bench scraper, just like the one that had been used to kill Patrick Black.

"So, Miss Gould," I began. "You're a hard woman to track down. Is there a reason you're so good at hiding?"

"Yeah, it's called smart publicity," Molly said glibly. "As soon as I heard about Patrick's death, I knew it was going to be a nightmare for me. His fanbase are rabid, they already put me through the wringer once before, I knew for sure it wouldn't be long until someone put a question mark next to my name and made me look guilty. I've been laying low and keeping my nose out until you guys figure out who actually did this."

"So you're saying you're innocent?" Blake asked.

"Uh, yeah," she said, her expression suggesting she thought the question stupid. "What evidence do you have on the contrary?"

"We know that you went through a messy public breakup with Black," Hudson said. "Very messy from what we hear. That alone puts you in the suspect chair. Several people that we spoke to mentioned your name."

"I was only at that party under the recommendation of my agent," Molly said. "Bernard Blasco was there, and rumor has it he wants me for his upcoming sci-fi blockbuster. I didn't even see Patrick. All in all, it was a great night—until the murder of course."

"What are you working on here?" I asked, nodding at the patisserie.

"Jacques is an award-winning patisserie chef; he's preparing things for tonight. He's been teaching me, sometimes I help him."

"That sort of thing requires a steady hand," I observed.

"Oh definitely. I love it though. Jacques says I've really taken to it."

"She is a natural," Jacques said affectionately. "My American diamond."

Blake stood up then and patted at his pockets aimlessly. "Say," he said to Jacques and Molly. "Do either of you have a cigarette I could steal? I'm in need of a nicotine hit."

Jacques shook his head and even grimaced a little. "No, cigarettes are disgusting. I have dedicated my life to pursuing the creation of flavor, why would I poison my tongue with that bile?" He paused. "No offense."

"None taken," Hudson said cordially. "How about you?"

Molly shook her head in a similar fashion. "No, my body is a temple. I don't smoke, drink, or do drugs. I exercise three times a day! Jacques and I are very health conscious. The only guilty pleasures we have are the things we make in here."

Hudson glanced at me, slapped his knee and sat back down. "Guess I'll have to wait a little while longer then for that hit."

"Miss Gould is there anyone *you* could think of that might have reason to hurt Patrick Black?" Blake asked.

"Pfft, the list is long, but I'm sure you know that by now. I heard one of his ex-security guards did it, have you checked that out?" Molly twirled her blonde hair in a tight curl.

"We've already ruled that one out," Hudson said with assurance. "Are there any names that come to mind for you though?"

She thought about it for a moment and shook her head. "No, honestly. Patrick was pretty horrible to most people, so I'm not surprised something like this happened to him. It was a matter of time to be honest. I'm sad it happened of course, but at the same time... he couldn't expect to get away with treating people like that forever, right?"

"I did a little reading up on you on the way over here," I said.

"Oh?" Molly replied with an intrigued turn of her head.

"You put up this image of being a bit of a blonde bimbo, but according to your Wikipedia page you have a PhD in Nuclear Physics."

"That's right," she said with a firm nod. "I also speak three languages, but I learned rather quickly that people would rather give money to a pretty woman pretending to be dumb, rather than a pretty woman that could hold her own in conversation."

"So that's where I've been going wrong," I muttered.

"Sprichst du Deutsch?" Hudson asked her. I looked at him in surprise. "What? I thought I'd search the web for a few phrases after all that grief you've given us."

"Ja, ich spreche Deutsch," she answered.

"And French, and the mandarin," Jacques chipped in from his corner. "My girlfriend is a very accomplished woman. A very sexy *and* accomplished woman."

"Jacques!" Molly said, smacking him playfully on the arm.

"Will you excuse us for a moment?" Blake said. "My colleagues and I would like to talk privately in the other room."

Molly, looking like she was done with it all, just shrugged her shoulders with indifference. "Whatever. I just want this out of my hair."

The three of us left the room, Hudson and I turning to regard Blake. "What's up?" I asked him.

"It was her," he said, his eyes glimmering with determination.

"What makes you sure?"

"It all adds up. She speaks German, there's a freaking bench scraper right there on the counter, she's got a steady hand and—"

"And she doesn't smoke cigarettes," Hudson interrupted. "The killer left a cigarette at the crime scene."

"Oh, come on, anyone can lie about that! She could be a smoker in secret!" Blake said, throwing his hands in the air.

"Just playing devil's advocate," Hudson eased. "For what it's worth I'm with you on this one. Zora, what about you?"

I bit my lip as I considered the question. "I'll admit she's our strongest suspect so far, but let's not jump the gun here. I'm not fully convinced—let's go back in there. I have a few more questions to ask."

We did go back in, but the questions I had loaded in my mind didn't come to fruition, as Molly Gould was standing proudly with a phone held up beside her, a large grin across her face. "I am such an idiot," she beamed. "I had proof this whole time that I'm innocent, and I didn't even realize."

"Please, indulge us," I said as we walked back to the counter.

"Thank god for live streaming, am I right?" she said as she thrust the phone in front of us. A video was playing, and from the looks of things it took place the night of Patrick Black's party.

"What are we looking at here?" Blake asked. "This some sort of live surveillance feed?"

Hudson slapped his forehead. "Blake... just... just leave the tech stuff to the adults."

"This is a stream from Johan Gutias—he was the DJ at Black's party. He had a camera on the crowd all night. You can see me over there in that corner, talking to Bernard Blasco. I was there with him the whole evening."

"My baby is going to be a film star," Jacques said proudly while balancing wafer rings on top of one another.

"Uh, can we get a copy of this video?" Hudson asked.

"Just go on Johan's channel. There's a copy of the video on there—it's like three hours long."

I clasped my hands on Hudson and Blake shoulders and smiled gleefully. "Well boys this is where I tap out. Looks like you've got a hefty piece of evidence to scour through. Call me and let me know when it's done. The bakery's close by, so I'll just walk back from here."

With that I started walking out of the kitchen, Blake calling after me as I left. "I thought you were going to help us with this!"

"The interesting parts, yeah!"

Scouring through a three-hour video of a DJ set to try and find a lead in an otherwise dead investigation? I'd leave that white knuckle action with Blake and Hudson.

CHAPTER 20

I dedicated the remainder of the day to drawing a firm line under my business with Nana Bucktooth. I'd solved her missing Moon Juice problem, but still not been to see her in person. After a short drive over to Wildwood I pulled up outside her wood paneled Victorian house in the forest and knocked on the front door.

"What do you want?" a gravelly voice on the other side said. I recognized it as the voice of Scrag, Nana Bucktooth's mangey familiar.

"It's Zora Wick, open up. I'm here to talk with Bucktooth."

The lock clicked and the door swung open on squeaking hinges, revealing the dark and dirty hallway. Scrag was sitting in a fruit bowl on the telephone table, somehow looking even worse than last time. I stepped inside and took a steadying breath—the aroma of dust and old wood hit me.

"Want a cup of tea?" Scrag croaked.

"That would be lovely actu—" I began, but he cut me off.

"Get one yourself then!" he yapped, laughing wildly at his 'joke'.

I scowled at him. "Where is Bucktooth? I need to speak to her."

"She's in the office upstairs, looking over the books."

"Okay, where is the office?" I asked. "This is a pretty big house."

"What do I look like? A talking map? You've got eyes, don't you? I'm sure you'll find it."

"You're just a real delight, eh?" I said as I walked past the horrible little cat. I placed my foot on the first stair and the wood squeaked heavily under my weight.

"By the way, one of those steps is cursed," Scrag said and cackled darkly. "I hope you don't step on it!"

"I'll step on you in a minute if you don't quiet down," I grumbled.

I figured there *wasn't* actually a cursed step and that the cat was messing with me, but to be honest he had successfully wormed his way into my head, so I took the stairs fours steps at a time to lower my odds of potentially being cursed.

At the top I found a sprawling landing that had corridors leading left, right, and center. Old, framed photographs covered the walls, and the house was stiflingly quiet, apart from the occasional creak of an old joist.

I held my fingers up in front of me to feel for the presence of magical energy and felt a faint trace from the corridor ahead of me. I walked its length entirely and at the end found it too split left and right.

"This place is a gosh darn maze," I muttered to myself. Looking left however I saw an open door with a light coming out of it. It was dark inside the house, given the fact that it was still light outside. I approached the slightly open door, knocked, and a voice came from inside.

"Come in," Bucktooth said coldly.

Pushing open the door I found a small study with a large mahogany desk at its center. Tall bookshelves lined each wall, each shelf crammed to the brim with books, papers, and files. A large taxidermy bear stood on its rear legs in the corner behind the old woman, its glassy black eyes appearing to look in two different directions. Bucktooth was sitting at the desk with miniscule reading glasses on the end of her nose and a large white quill in her hand, an old book the size of a tabletop open in front of her.

The book's pages were old yellow parchment and scrawled upon them in ink there appeared to be some sort of very complicated ledger, written in tiny lettering. The old woman scratched her quill over the paper carefully, adding something to the incomparable volume.

"What is that?" I asked, unable to contain my curiosity.

"This is the book for Brewer Family Distribution Ltd. The same book my father bought when he started the business over a century ago."

"You do all your records by hand?" I gasped. "There is software now, computers take care of that stuff in seconds!"

Bucktooth looked up at me momentarily and scowled. "Computers will be the death of man, you'll see." Bucktooth added another nimble entry, her tongue sticking slightly out the corner of her mouth. "What did you want?"

"I came here to tell you that the business with the Moon Juice is done. We found the thieves." After a paused I added, "To be honest Zelda is the one that did most of the work. I was just there for the ride."

"I'm aware," she said in a bored manner, not looking up from her work. "But you're being there did have a purpose—she comes out of her cage more when you're there."

"I can't disagree with that." Zelda had been a whirlwind these past couple of days in Wildwood. I'd never seen anything like it.

"So, is that all you came to say?" Bucktooth asked. "Or was there something else you wanted?"

"Uh…" I drawled, a little taken back by the reaction. I hadn't expected any great thanks, but at least some sort of recognition. "The curse between Hudson and Blake. Can you please break it?"

The old woman looked pained by the idea, but she huffed. "I suppose I gave you my word that I would. Tell me, did they kill one another?"

"No, the opposite actually. I think they're friends now."

"And do you think that will last once the curse is over?" she asked with a note of intrigue.

"I hope so," I said after a moment's consideration. "Things are much better this way. They're always at each other's throats."

She nodded. "That's in their nature. As your guardian each of them is fated to fall in love with you, and you with them. The unusual thing is having more than one guardian, but *you'll* have to find a way of dealing with that mess."

I laughed awkwardly. "I'm not in love with them, and they're not in love with me."

"Cut the crap darling, I don't have time for lies. I can see the truth in you, even if you don't know it yourself yet. Every powerful witch I've ever known with a guardian ended up marrying them—heck, I married mine."

"You had a guardian?" I said in astonishment.

"Certainly did. Llewyn Fox. We had twenty good years together before he got killed by The Sisters of Shade. He died saving me."

"I'm sorry, I had no idea."

Bucktooth continued to add to the ledger, neither her face nor voice betraying any hint of emotion. "Well, that was a long time ago. My point is this—hurry up and pick one of them. You stand around waiting for life to start, but here's the thing: the clock's always been ticking. None of us is getting any younger, and before you know it the man you loved is lying dead in your arms and you wished you'd gotten even just one more day."

"I... I..."

Nana Bucktooth set her quill down, sat back in her chair and steepled her fingers. "You were born with a great curse—being a prismatic witch. I wouldn't wish that even upon my worst enemy. With your abilities you will reach power the likes of which most will never know, but with that gift comes the burden of expectation. You think trouble has noticed you yet? Girl... things haven't even started. Word is already spreading through our would about you, and it won't be long before the masses come. Dealing with the Sisters of the Shade will be one thing, but there are others out there, and you're going to have to deal with them all."

"Right," I said after a moment's consideration. "Why are you telling me all of this?"

Bucktooth sighed. "I don't know. You're not going to pay attention to half of it anyway. You can go now; I've got a lot to take care of."

I turned then to walk out the door but stopped and looked back at her. "Don't you want to know who stole the Moon Juice?"

"It was Will Hackerty and Billy Brewer. I knew all along," she said with disinterest. "They're doping up that Moon Bear of theirs."

"Wait, you knew all along?" I asked. "Why have us look into it then?"

"Girl, ain't a thing happens in this town that I don't know about. I wanted to see how you and Zelly would cope with something small time. The fact of the matter is that bigger problems are lurking on the horizon, and I needed to know that I've got the tools to deal with them." Bucktooth pulled out a cigarette and lit it. "What can I say? Congratulations, you passed the test." She snapped her fingers. "The curse is broken on your boyfriends. Now get out of here and try not to get yourself killed. I'll have use for you again real soon."

With that I left Nana Bucktooth's house feeling confused and mystified. A stranger person I had yet to meet, and with every encounter the old woman only became more of an enigma. For now at least my business with her was done, though something told me our relationship was only just beginning.

What that meant in the long run, I could only begin to imagine.

* * *

TO MY SURPRISE the next few days actually passed without incident. The case had hit a decided dead-end and Hudson and Blake had made no progress with their three hours of DJ footage, so I went back to the bakery and spent some time on the retail frontlines with Daphne and Rosie.

I'd just closed up the shop on Tuesday and said goodbye to the girls when Sabrina came into the kitchen through the bakery back door. She had both her hands held behind her back, and a roguish grin upon her face.

"Oh dear," I smirked while tidying up the last of the day's things. "That grin seems troublesome. What's going on?"

"What's going on is that you only have the best cousin in the world," Sabrina said and produced a wand made of white wood that seemed to glow under the kitchen lights.

"Oh my goodness, it's beautiful," I gasped. "Is that my new wand?"

"Certainly is," she said and handed it to me. Straightaway the white wood grew warm to my touch and under the surface motes of rainbow color twisted around the body. I felt a huge charge of energy sweep up my arm and move through me.

"It's powerful!" I puffed. "Quite intense actually!"

"That's just because you've not been using magic properly for a few days. You'll probably have to release a couple blasts of raw energy to keep yourself from boiling over. You can send a blast straight into the sky or..." Sabrina looked around the kitchen quickly and grabbed a small cauldron from off the side. "Or fire into here!" She turned the cauldron on its side and took a cautionary step back.

"Just point and fire into the cauldron?" I asked. "You're sure?"

Sabrina nodded. "Yeah, it's safe. The cauldron will absorb the force."

I lifted the quaking wand and pointed the tip at the cauldron. Although I'd never done this before I instinctively knew what to do. It was like I was opening a valve and letting water blast out from a dam, but the water was the overwhelming build of magic inside me.

I let the energy out, and it left the wand as a cataclysmic blast of light that roared across the kitchen. It hit the cauldron with a blinding flash and continued for a few seconds until I felt like it was done.

I lowered the wand, my whole-body trembling with adrenaline. The cauldron was glowing white hot from the force, and as I looked over at Sabrina, I saw her mouth was wide open.

"...Okay, I've never seen one quite like that before, but still... that must feel better, right?"

"Much better," I said, feeling slightly out of breath. I pressed the tip of my wand into the palm of my hand and stored it safely in my aura. It felt good to have a wand again, it was strangely comforting in a way.

"Not to brag but that's the best wand I've ever made," Sabrina said proudly. "You won't be able to break that thing easily, it's reinforced with crystallized moon light—you don't even want to know what I had to do to get my hands on that. Nearly blew apart the wand lathe making this baby."

"Thank you, Sabrina, seriously. I mean it. How much do I owe you?"

"Zora you are family, so it's on the house. I only ask that you pay me back with an unlimited supply of baked goods around the clock."

I laughed. "Hey, fill your boots," I said, pointing at the few unsold bakes left from the day. Sabrina squealed with joy and immediately devoured four eclairs. It was only then that I noticed there was something inside the cauldron, a black human skull with bright blue flames in its eye sockets. "What the heck?!" I gasped. Sabrina, her mouth still full, turned around to see the skull too.

"Was that there when I turned the cauldron over?" she asked.

"No, no it wasn't," I said.

The blue flames moved around the skull's eyes sockets, as though it was taking in the room. Then its mouth started moving as it talked. "Where am I?!" it said in a panicked voice. Both Sabrina and I grabbed hold of each other and jumped back in alarm. "It talked!" I squeaked.

"Who said that? Who said that?!" the blue-eyed skull barked.

"Holy moly, it's an Oracle," Sabrina said.

"Who is that?!" the skull shrieked. "Who said that?!"

"Stop shouting, we're over here," Sabrina said, waving her arm. The blue flames flickered our way and the expressionless skull found us.

"Who are you? Where am I? What's happening?!" the skull rasped.

Sabrina nudged me to answer. "Uh, I'm Zora Wick, this is my cousin Sabrina. You're in Compass Cove. I don't know what you're doing in my cauldron… though it probably has something to do with me." I turned and whispered to Sabrina. "What is this thing? Are we in trouble?"

She shook her head. "It's an Oracle. They're very old spirits embodied in the form of a skull. Supposedly they have vast magical knowledge—I don't know why it's in your cauldron though." She looked at the skull. "What's your name?"

"Doesn't work like that," the skull said abruptly. "Whoever summoned me here needs to give me a name. I'm going to need one now that I live here."

"Can't you just go back to the place where you came from?" I asked.

The talking skull couldn't really show emotion, but the way its jaw opened told me it found that question highly offensive. "Lady let me give you a little background on me. I was servant to Layla the Terrible for three centuries, then some guy killed her, and I've been in the void ever since. I was happily minding my own business with some shame demons on the rings of Neptune when a bolt of magic ripped me across the cosmos and brought me here!"

"I think he's saying this is a permanent thing," Sabrina muttered.

"No offense Mr. Skull, but I really don't need any more... pets?" I wasn't quite sure what word fit here. Either way, Artemis and Phoebe were already enough for me to handle.

"Well maybe you should think about that before releasing a blast of energy into the cosmos and summoning a great and powerful being!" the skull scolded. "Look you brought me here so I'm in your servitude for your life. If you don't want me here, then you have to kill me. I'll quite happily take a hammer. Just make it quick and do it from behind."

"What the heck dude, I'm not going to kill you!" I said, sharing a look of disbelief with Sabrina.

"Then I guess I'm here to stay. Woo," the skull said flatly. "Now do you have a name for me or what?"

"What was your last name?" Sabrina asked helpfully.

"Layla the Terrible named me Zagoflax. It means 'Blood Flayer' in old demonic. I'm not allowed to reuse names though."

"...Right," Sabrina said, looking as lost as I felt.

"So, name?" it prompted.

I stared at the skull for a moment before letting out a very long sigh. "Uh, I don't know... how about Bill?" I said with uncertainty. I'd never named a talking skull before.

"Doesn't sound very fancy," the skull observed.

"Okay, how about 'Fancy Bill'?"

"I love it. Fancy Bill I am. What's the first item of business then? Impaling armies on bone pyres? Weaving blankets from human flesh?"

"This is a bakery. I sell cakes and baked goods."

"Uh... right then," Fancy Bill said hesitantly. "Not a problem, as an Oracle I'm completely neutral. I adapt to my current master's whims! What kind of things did you have in mind for me?"

"Honestly, I didn't mean to summon you. I was just releasing some excess magical energy."

Fancy Bill stared at me with his mouth hanging open. "Layla the Terrible sacrificed one thousand humans, stole the blood stone from Zana Guth, and harnessed the power of lightning to summon me—and you're telling me you brought me here by accident?"

I laughed nervously. "Welcome to the team?"

"For a blank skull he looks awfully underwhelmed right now," Sabrina muttered in my ear.

I wasn't sure if it wasn't underwhelmed, or just complete disbelief at my sheer ineptitude. Regardless, *I* was responsible for bringing this talking skull here, and it seemed he needed some sort of purpose. "I don't suppose you're any good at solving mysteries? That tends to happen quite a lot around here."

Fancy Bill scoffed, and in a haughty manner he asked, "You're asking if I, an Oracle with access to the infinite knowledge of the cosmos, know anything about solving mysteries?"

"Yes, that's one way of putting it I suppose."

His voice dimmed. "To be honest they've always been a bit of a weak spot for me. You've got to have the brain for that sort of thing, you know?"

"Great," I said, slapping my hands on my thighs. "Well, when I think of a task for you, I'll let you know. Until then… I'll have to find a spot for you. I'm thinking Constance's old room." Somewhere Fancy Bill would be out of the way.

"Constance, eh? Was she some sort of great and dark powerful witch too?" Fancy Bill asked with glee.

"Just for the record we're all good witches around here. Are you sure you're neutral?" Sabrina asked suspiciously. "Dark masters seem to be a recurrent theme for you."

"I just go where I'm summoned lady," Fancy Bill said flippantly. "It's not my fault my masters tend to be of the evil variety. I don't choose where I go."

"He's got a point there," I said to Sabrina.

She blinked at me for a few seconds before turning. "Well, it looks like the wand is working. I'm going to go home, back to my house that doesn't have an evil talking skull."

"Not evil!" Fancy Bill called to her as she left the room.

"No such thing as a bad dog, am I right?" I said to the skull, determined to give him a chance.

He stared at me with his lifeless blue flames flickering away. "What the frig is that supposed to mean, lady?"

"It's an expression. It means that the owner is responsible and not —you know what why am I explaining this to you? I thought you were some sort of all-knowing cosmic entity."

"You try knowing everything in the universe. It takes time to sift through that infinite garbage heap. If it's idioms you want though I'll start working on it!" Suddenly Fancy Bill's eyes went out and a gust of wind swept across the counter.

This was definitely one of my weirder Tuesdays.

CHAPTER 21

After tidying up the bakery I went upstairs and grabbed a quick bite to eat before my magic class. About an hour before I was due to leave an envelope squeezed through the living room windows and floated across the apartment to land on the kitchen table.

I was eating a bowl of noodles and watched in doubt as the letter wrangled itself form the envelope and folded into an intricate origami figurine of my magic teacher, Amos Aposhine.

"Just a quick note to say that the magic class will be held at Compass Cove Community College until further notice, due to unexpected renovations at the usual venue. The class will be listed under 'Accounting Theory'. This message will now self-destruct."

I pushed my chair back to run away and the paper figuring of Amos swan dived off the table and burst into flame before hitting the floor. My bowl of noodles was still in my hand, and a trail of noodles were even dangling from my mouth. I slurped them up and put the bowl back on the table.

"Things were better without magic; things were better without magic..." I repeated to myself, vaguely recalling those halcyon days when life was mundane and somewhat predictable.

"Hermes in the house!" Hermes shouted as he jumped through the cat flap.

"Where have you been?" I asked, "I feel like I haven't seen you in days."

"Funny story actually. Tell me, what do you know about flamingoes?"

"I really haven't got time for this. I've got magic school tonight. Just having a quick bite to eat before I have to leave."

He rolled his eyes and huffed. "Spoil sport. By the way did you know there is an Oracle in your kitchen?"

"Yeah, I summoned him here by accident when testing out my new wand. He's… interesting to say the least."

"Which Oracle is it? There's only like a handful of those guys, I might know him."

"He's calling himself 'Fancy Bill' now, but he said in his previous iteration he served someone called 'Layla the Terrible'."

Hermes nodded slowly. "Ah Layla, there's someone I've not thought about for a couple hundred years. I tell you what those were the good old days. She was a mad old broad."

"Good old days?" I said and slurped up more noodles. "Fancy Bill said this woman killed thousands of humans."

"Oh, she did," he said with a serious turn. "But they don't really make villains like that today, you know what I mean? Back then magic was wild, like *really* wild. Not tame like it is now."

"I'll take tame over magical genocide."

"I was one of the wizards that tried to stop her you know? The armies of men allied to stop the dark witch queen. She blew my arm off with a bolt of lightning." Hermes tutted and chuckled to himself as though recalling a much cheerier story. "Would you believe it was a human that got her in the end? Claymore right through the spine. Whammy! Ah, those were the days."

The noodles dripped off my fork and splashed back into the bowl. "It worries me that we share a bed sometimes."

"Phone!" Phoebe squawked from her perch. "It's Hudson."

Sure enough my phone started buzzing across the kitchen table, I picked it up and answered. "Hey."

"I don't suppose you've somehow solved this case without telling us," Hudson sighed.

"Ha, I'm afraid not. Are things really that bad?"

"We've been shadowing Molly Gould and Mitchell Murphy to see if we might find something interesting, but they're the most boring suspects ever. Gould barely leaves her boyfriend's restaurant, and the only interesting place Murphy went was to the community college for a night class, but that's hardly relevant."

"Coffee, it's a class about coffee," Blake said in the background. "He's duller than dishwater."

"Blake's there with you?" I asked Hudson.

"Yeah, we figured two minds were better than one."

"You know the curse is broken now, I told you that. You guys don't have to live in each other's pockets anymore."

Hudson made a weird grunt. "We know that. Once this case is over, we'll go our separate ways."

"...Right, it just kind of feels like you two are actually friends now."

Hudson laughed. "Friends with that idiot? Think again. Anyway, we were wondering if we could pick you up to do some more sleuthing with us. We're out of angles, but you usually always think of something."

"No can do sorry, I've got magic class tonight. Actually, it's at the community college too, if I bump into Mitchell Murphy I can always try and pry some more information out of him—he might be able to give us a lead."

"Don't hold your breath, but okay. I'll speak to you tomorrow."

"Later."

After I finished my noodles, I got ready and left for class, driving my van over to the community college. The parking lot was quite full and as I entered the foyer, I had to sign a registration. I put my name under the class for 'Accounting Theory' and out of curiosity I checked the register under 'Espresso 101' for Mitchell's name. To my surprise it wasn't there, but under another class instead: 'Bread Making for Beginners.'

Huh.

As I followed the signs to the room for Amos' class, I pulled out my phone and called Blake.

"Hey, what's up?" he asked.

"When I spoke to Hudson earlier you said Mitchell Murphy went to night school for a coffee class."

"Yeah, we saw a list of classes on the school's website and assumed that would be the one."

"Did you check though? Because I've just seen his name under Bread Making for beginners."

"Okay? Do you want me to arrest him for that?" Blake asked.

"Don't be a jerk about it. I just thought it might be relevant."

"Sneak in there and see what's going on then. He *did* tell us he knew nothing about baking. Seems like we caught him in a small lie. It might mean something."

"Alright, I'll let you know."

With that I carried on down the hall to Amos' room. As I did, I passed a room with one long glass wall. On the other side there was a large kitchen and rows of students all kneading dough at various benches. Right at the back I saw Mitchell Murphy.

I hurried past the window to avoid being seen and ducked into Amos' room. Amos was already there, and so were Neil and Jane, my fellow students. "Ah, Zora! Good of you to join us again. Sorry about the venue change, we're trying to repair the hole your rhino made, but it just keeps undoing itself! Some weird magic there."

"Sorry," I said, feeling a pang of awkward guilt as I took a seat next to Jane and Neil. "I've got a new wand now; I can try and fix it?"

"Uh no, no!" he said, looking rather panicked by the idea. "No that's okay, I'll get it sorted. Anyway, I'd like to welcome you all to our first magical theory class. As we're in a human space we won't be doing any actual magic tonight, but we've got something much more interesting to cover—the *theory* behind the magic."

Amos turned to his desk and picked up three huge identical books and slammed them down in front of us. It was a large brown leather-bound book with a small white title at the top. *Theory of Magic Volume 1: Edition 923. First published in 1432 by Edward Blathersby.*

"Now if you'll all turn to page 408, we have a rather exciting chapter arguing the various definitions of magic."

Neil and Jane seemed somewhat excited, but as I turned to the relevant page and saw the entire book was lines and lines of printed text so tiny that it was almost illegible, I found myself sinking in my chair.

"The year is 1604," Amos read from the chapter. "The witch Amelia Druit wrote in a letter to Meg the black, *'Magic is like the color brown. But how do we define brown? To me brown is...'*"

Unfortunately, I never got to hear what Amelia Druit thought of the color brown, because I fell asleep within the first five seconds of Amos talking. When I next opened my eyes again it was because Amos had slammed his copy of the book shut.

"Alright then, what a thrilling thirty-minute introduction! I think we should all pause for a quick bathroom break and then we'll get right back to it!"

"Absolutely mental, isn't it?" Neil asked me. "I had no idea the theory behind this stuff was so interesting."

"Uh yeah," I said, wiping drool off my face as I sat up. "It's really *mental*. Excuse me, I'm just going to go to the bathroom." I hopped out of my chair and quickly left the room, eager to avoid being drawn into any more conversation about magical theory. It seemed no one had noticed I'd fallen asleep—clearly, they'd been too absorbed in the riveting lesson.

As I walked down the hallway I passed the bread making class and saw Mitchell Murphy once more. An idea came to me then and I jogged into the women's bathroom, found a stall and called Zelda.

"Can I use magic to change my face?" I asked her.

"Oh, come on Zora, don't be so hard on yourself. There's nothing wrong with your face!"

"I'm talking about a disguise, you nitwit!"

"Ah. Nothing springs to mind to be honest. What are you up to?"

"I want to talk to a suspect without them knowing it's me," I explained.

"Well using any sort of magic to change your physical appearance is highly dangerous and I do not recommend you do it. That's coming from the girl that accidentally turned her hair white."

Good point. "Alright you may be onto something with that one."

"I mean you could always try the Clark Kent classic and take your glasses off. Maybe put a hat on too? You'd be surprised how a few small changes can make your face look different. I got banned from that coffee shop on Main Avenue because they said I was staring at that hot barista guy, well I went back in without my glasses on and it totally worked for like an hour. They did end up kicking me out again."

"...I find myself constantly surprised that you volunteer these stories to me without a second thought."

"That story demonstrated my cunning initiative, I have nothing to be embarrassed about!" she wailed.

"I think we're having a conversation about boundaries the next time I see you. Anyway, got to go. Later!" I hung up the phone, pulled out my wand and magicked up a few small items for my 'big transformation'.

I had a beret, a scarf, and once I took my glasses off and looked in the mirror I must admit I did look quite different, but I really wasn't sure if it was a big enough change that Murphy wouldn't recognize me. Making sure that I was alone in the room I pulled out my wand again, pointed it at my glasses and tried to make them darker so they'd act more like sunshades.

My wand glowed bright with colorful light and a charge shot out of it then, but instead of hitting my glasses it narrowly missed, ricocheted off the counter, bounced off the mirror and hit me right in the middle of my face. "Son of a—!" I reeled, twisting away from the mirror and holding my nose.

When I looked at myself again, I found myself staring at someone completely different. A girl that looked almost Mediterranean in appearance, with olive-skin and a small button nose. Irritatingly the new face was much more attractive than my usual one.

Zelda's warnings of not using magic to tamper with my appearance floated through my mind. I felt a little sick at having accidentally done such drastic magic, but the 'damage' was done now so to speak, so I pushed the worry down and tried not to think about it.

That's the way to do it!

I headed for the bread making class and went inside. "Excuse me, am I too late?" I asked.

"No, come on in," the teacher said from the front. "We're near the end so you can pair up and watch tonight. Pick a table."

Naturally I went straight over to Mitchell's counter. He was the closest to me anyway as he was at the back of the pack. "Mind if I join?" I asked.

"Be my guest," he said, looking rather flustered. *Clearly Mitchell likes Zora 2.0 more than the old one.* Mitchell and the rest of the class were currently dividing up dough into small balls and rolling it over the counter with their hands acting like little cages. "We're making rolls tonight," he said. "Do you want a go?"

"Oh, I'd probably mess it up. I'm happy to watch you for now. Have you been doing this long?"

"A few months," Mitchell answered. "It's very therapeutic."

"What's that for?" I said, eyeing the metallic bench scraper on the counter. It was identical to the one found at the crime scene.

"This? You can use it for scraping dough off the counter or chopping. Pretty handy," he said, offering a flirtatious grin. "Just be careful though. They can be sharp."

"Very nice Mitchell," the teacher said as he came over to inspect his progress. He looked up at me and smiled. "What's your name?"

"Nora," I gulped, wishing I'd thought of a fake name before coming in here. "Nora… Dough."

The teacher's genial smile faded a little as I gave the obvious fake name. "…Okay, Nora. Are you interested in joining the class? Like I said you're a bit late to do anything tonight, but next session you can jump straight in. It's $15 for each class, and all the equipment is provided upfront. That doesn't mean you take it home though, eh Mitchell?"

Mitchell laughed in familiarity and looked at me in explanation. "I have a bad habit of mindlessly putting things in my pockets without realizing. In my defense I always bring stuff back."

"Watch your purse around this one!" the teacher jested. "Anyway, good to meet you, Nora. Speak with me after class if you're interested."

"So, you're a thief?" I joked to Mitchell. He rolled his eyes but smiled at me.

"No, just absent minded. Look." He reached into his pockets and pulled out a thermometer, a fork, and a small book on looking after bonsai trees. "I don't even have a bonsai tree. I don't know where half of this stuff comes from. My mom says I've done it ever since I was a kid.

"She was a stand-in doctor, so we were always moving around between different houses. One time I left my favorite toy and only realized when it was too late, I was distraught, never got it back. After that I made sure I always had important things in my pockets... soon it just became anything old thing."

"You must have lived in a lot of different states then," I said.

"Nah, we did most of the moving around when I was little actually, in Europe. My mother is from Germany originally, we moved to America when I—argh!"

Mitchell was in the middle of dividing more dough up when he slipped and caught the side of his hand with the metal blade. He'd been so busy talking to me he hadn't been paying attention properly. Right away he drew back his hand and gripped his wrist to stop the bleeding—and there was quite a lot of blood.

"Are you okay?" I asked him.

"I'm fine," he said with a determined smile. He wrapped his hand with a kitchen towel and didn't look too bothered. It was the smallest thing, but at that moment it all came together for me.

"So, you were faking back in the apartment," I said out loud. "Probably because you felt like we were already too close."

"Excuse me?" he said in confusion.

"I must admit the bench scraper had me stumped for the longest time. Why on earth would someone have one of those on them? A very random thing to carry around. After hearing your little story then about your nomadic childhood, it makes more sense—especially given your habit of putting random things in your pockets."

"Do I know you?" he said, his eyes narrowing.

"And I suppose the bit about your mother being a stand-in doctor is revealing too. You must have picked a thing or two from her about the human body. That's why you slashed him right across the carotid artery. You knew exactly where to strike."

Murphy took a step back from the counter and looked at me like I was speaking in French. "You…"

"The cigarette at the crime scene was simple enough. You smoke like a chimney. I'm guessing the German book you took was an heirloom of your childhood. But the real question is why? Why did you do it?"

"Who the hell are you?" he demanded, his hands curling into fists.

I ignored the question. "I'm guessing you went up to his room to speak, and he *did* ask you to write more songs for him, but the offer would only be insulting. Probably offered you another measly percentage on top of what he already offered you out of court. It was your work after all. Why should he reap all the rewards and get away with the praise that so rightly belonged to you?"

"There was no offer," Murphy growled quietly. "He demanded that I give him more songs for free. Said I should be grateful for the opportunity."

"And that's when you snapped. You never went up there with the intention of harming him. But you grabbed the first thing you found in your pocket and sliced it across his throat. You were so overcome with adrenaline you threw it in the sink straightaway, had a cigarette to still your nerves and figured you'd steal the book before you realized you had to get the heck out of there."

"You're wrong about one thing actually. The book. Not a heirloom from my childhood. That was the book I kept my music and lyrics in. It's the one he stole from me."

"Mitchell Murphy, I'm placing you under arrest for the murder of—"

Before I could finish the sentence Murphy hurled his tray of unbaked dough at me and it hit me square in the face. I threw my arms up to block the blow, but it still sent me crashing onto my ass.

"Get back here!" I shouted and jumped back up to my feet. Everyone else in the classroom had turned around to see what the commotion was, but I was past caring. I bolted out of the room after Murphy, who was quickly making his getaway. "Stop!" I shouted after him as I skidded into the main hallway. "It's over, Mitchell!"

Mitchell kept running but turned back briefly, and an expression of confusion was fixed upon his face. "Wait a minute, you?!"

Confused myself, I looked at my reflection in the glass window of the kitchen classroom and saw my face was back to normal. *Uh oh, explain that one Zora. Your face just magically changed.*

"Uh... prosthetics!" I said quickly. "You knocked them off. That was assault by the way! Now stop!"

"Go to hell!" Murphy said before bolting out of the doors and into the parking lot. "That jerk had it coming to him! The world's a better place without him!"

A few seconds later I burst out of the door too and skidded to a halt. There was zero sign of Murphy anywhere. Then I heard his voice behind me. He'd hidden at the side of the entrance just after sprinting out. He had picked up a large rock from a decorative gravel border by the wall and was walking towards me slowly. "Look, don't take this personally, but I'm not about to lose my life over that dirtbag. I'm sorry, but you know too much."

"Don't do this Mitchell!" I pleaded, stepping back slowly as I watched him lift up the rock. There was only a few feet between us and I had no chance of getting away. As soon as that rock hit my head it would be game over.

"There's no other way. Sorry."

He swung his arms down to deliver the blow and in that split second I pulled out my wand and let another blast of wild magic loose. A beam of white light exploded from the tip and sent Mitchell's body hurling through the glass doors and into the foyer of the community college. He hit the ground and was still—knocked unconscious from the ferocious magical explosion.

I fell onto the ground, my breath heaving at having come so close to death. My hands were trembling from adrenaline. It was over, I'd caught Patrick Black's killer. Lying down on the ground I pulled out my phone and called Hudson.

"Zora. How's magic theory class going?"

"Pretty badly, but I did solve the case. It was Murphy. He's currently lying unconscious in the foyer of the community college. Come arrest him?"

"We'll be right there!" Hudson said, suddenly sounding more serious.

I breathed a sigh of relief knowing it was over with.

Maybe now I could finally get a bit of peace.

CHAPTER 22

"Not in my room, get it out!" Constance moaned. "I don't want that thing in there!"

I went to set Fancy Bill down on Constance's side table but huffed at her protest. "Will you relax? Fancy Bill is part of this family now, and we need a nice quiet place to put him. You're never in your room, so what's the problem?"

"The problem is that thing used to be a servant for Layla the Terrible! One of the worst witches of the last century might I add! There's no telling the horrible things that gruesome little skull did for her."

"Fine, I'll just shove him in the pantry."

After heading back downstairs to hide Fancy Bill in the pantry I came back up, walked into the kitchen and picked up my cup of tea. "Listen, he's neutral, so he follows the whim of whatever leader he has. He's currently researching all idioms and expressions in the universe, so I imagine he'll be asleep for quite a while."

Constance flopped down on the ground and crossed her arms. "I'm still not happy about it."

Later that evening Celeste and Sabrina came over for some Chinese food and a movie marathon. Zelda was absent as she apparently wasn't feeling well. This quickly came up in our conversation.

"She said what?" Celeste asked with intrigue. "When she left the café, I caught her in that cowgirl getup again!"

We all straightened up at having caught Zelda in her lie. "Wait, you don't think she's gone to Wildwood, do you?" Sabrina said excitedly.

I shrugged my shoulders. "I suppose it's a possibility. She said she left her ex because of his ways, but by all accounts, he does seem like a changed man."

"We should call her!" Hermes cackled. "Ask if she wants some lemon tea bringing over!"

"Let's leave her alone," I said to the mischievous little cat. "She obviously wants to keep it a secret, so let's try and respect that."

"I give her three days and then I'm bringing it up," Celeste said.

Sabrina scoffed. "No way you'll last three days."

After helping Daphne and Rosie with the bake the next morning I went over to the Magic Library to see if I could find out more about my mother and her mysterious research before she vanished. Upon getting there however I found a sign on the hidden entrance to the Magic Library—it was especially unusual because the library was usually never closed.

Closed due to emergency, back soon. Maybe.

"That's weird," I muttered to myself.

As I walked outside and started down the library's large stone steps, I stopped in surprise to see Hudson there. "Hey," I said slowly. The last time I'd saw him here he was leaving on a dangerous mission and told me he might never come back—*he of course did.*

"Hey, sorry to catch you by surprise. I just… well there's something I wanted to talk to you about."

"Okay?"

"I didn't get a lot of sleep last night because I was up thinking about it all, and—heck, I guess there's no easy way of saying it. So, I'll just say it. I like you. A lot, and if I hadn't read this situation wrong then I think maybe you like me too. I want to take you out for dinner, a nice dinner. And then maybe we can keep going out for nice dinners, and maybe we can only do that with each other, exclusively, if you know what I mean?"

It was amusing to see Hudson breaking down with nerves, as he was usually so calm and collected. There was a huge grin on my face, and I bit my lower lip. "I know what you mean, and I think I'd like to do that."

Hudson smiled too, and then he stepped forward and took me in his arms, kissing me as he did so. For a few moments it felt like I was floating off the ground, and as I looked down, I realized I *actually* was. I let out a small shriek and dropped to the ground, Hudson laughed too.

"Uh, we'll have to keep an eye on that, I don't want you floating away on me."

"Maybe you can tie some string around me, like a balloon?" I joked. A concern came to me then. "This isn't going to change things between you and Blake, is it?"

He shook his head. "No, we talked about it face to face. He actually told me to go for it. Said he wasn't ready for something serious."

"Huh," I said, wondering if he was okay.

The day after that I found out why Blake had said that. It was the end of the day at the bakery when he came through the front door, an unusual expression on his face.

"Hey stranger," I said. "Haven't seen you for a couple of days. Where have you been?"

"I had to go back to the forest on pack business," he said with an awkward smile. "Something came up."

"Everything okay back there?" I asked, noting that something felt a little off.

"Uh... it's fine. There was an unexpected development between packs, and... well—I had to do something."

I was feeling worried now. "Blake? What is it? Is something wrong?"

"Sometimes in my world you don't get to make choices. There are arrangements, arrangements that are made for the greater good. Wait here a second." Blake went to the front door of the bakery, stepped out onto the street and gestured for someone to come. A tall woman with long white hair came into view. She took Blake's hand and he led her inside the bakery. The woman next to him was classically beautiful, with an expression that was somehow kind and shrewd.

"Lori this is Zora, the person I've been charged with protecting. Zora this is Lori. As of yesterday, she is my wife."

My jaw about hit the floor. "I'm sorry, your wife? I didn't know you were seeing someone?!"

Lori smiled amicably. "Funny story, we weren't. We all have to make sacrifices though, don't we Blake?"

Blake raised his brows and looked back at me. "We're taking it one day at a time."

"I'm, I'm happy for you?" I said with uncertainty.

"Don't worry," Lori assured. "It's a shock for us as well. I hope we can be good friends though Zora, Blake has already told me a lot about you. Maybe you can tell me a thing or two about him, I certainly need it—we don't know a single thing about one another!"

"Sorry to drop this on you," Blake said. "I couldn't think of any other way."

"No, it's fine. It's…"

"Zora?" Rosie asked as she came into the kitchen holding Fancy Bill. "I just found this thing in the pantry. Is it yours?"

All of a sudden Fancy Bill's flaming blue eyes reignited. "Wow, weird energy in here Zora! Who are all these people? I'm done with that idiom research you wanted. Yowza! You could cut the tension in here with a knife!"

That was putting it lightly.

CLICK HERE to read Book 5: A Scone to Pick.

THANKS FOR READING

Thanks for reading, I hope you enjoyed the book.

It would really help me out if you could leave an honest review with your thoughts and rating on Amazon.

Every bit of feedback helps!

ALSO BY MARA WEBB

~ Ongoing ~

Hallow Haven Witch Mysteries

An English Enchantment

Compass Cove Cozy Mysteries

~ Completed ~

Wicked Witches of Pendle Island

Wildes Witches Mysteries

Raven Bay Mysteries

Wicked Witches of Vanish Valley

MAILING LIST

Want to be notified when I release my latest book? Join my mailing list. It's for new releases only. No spam:

Click here to join!

I'll also send you a free 120,000 word book as a thank you for signing up.

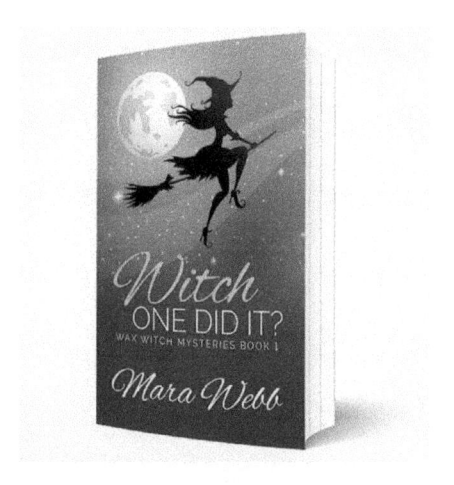

marawebbauthor.com

amazon.com/-/e/B081X754NL
facebook.com/marawebbauthor
twitter.com/marawebbauthor
bookbub.com/authors/mara-webb